How Like A God . . .

I turned on the screen and regarded the spirals of light, moving in both clockwise and counterclockwise directions about a point directly before me. These were the stars, visible only in this fashion, there, on the underside of space. As I hung there and the universe moved about me, I felt the decades' layers of fat that padded my soul's midsection catch fire and begin to burn. The man I had worked so hard at becoming died then, I hope, and I felt that Shimbo of Darktree Tower, Shrugger of Thunders, still lived.

I watched the spinning stars, grateful, sad and proud, as only a man who has outlived his destiny and realized he might yet forge himself another, can be.

After a time, the whirlpool in the sky sucked me down to sleep's dark center, dreamless and cool, soft and still, like the Valley of Shadows perhaps.

William

ISLE OF THE DEAD

ROGER ZELAZNY

BAEN
BOOKS

ISLE OF THE DEAD

Copyright © 1969 by Roger Zelazny

A Baen Books Original

Baen Publishing Enterprises
260 Fifth Avenue
New York, N.Y. 10001

ISBN: 0-671-72011-2

Cover art by John Rheaume

First Baen printing, August 1990

Distributed by
SIMON & SCHUSTER
1230 Avenue of the Americas
New York, N.Y. 10020

Printed in the United States of America

to Banks Mebane

I

LIFE IS A THING—if you'll excuse a quick dab of philosophy before you know what kind of picture I'm painting—that reminds me quite a bit of the beaches around Tokyo Bay.

Now, it's been centuries since I've seen that Bay and those beaches, so I could be off a bit. But I'm told that it hasn't changed much, except for the condoms, from the way that I remember it.

I remember a terrible expanse of dirty water, brighter and perhaps cleaner way off in the distance, but smelling and slopping and chill close at hand, like Time when it wears away objects, delivers them, removes them. Tokyo Bay, on any given day, is likely to wash anything ashore. You name it, and it spits it up some time or other: a dead man, a shell that might be alabaster, rose and pumpkin bright, with a sinistral whorling, rising inevitably to the tip of a horn as innocent as the unicorn's, a bottle with or without a note which

you may or may not be able to read, a human
foetus, a piece of very smooth wood with a nail
hole in it—maybe a piece of the True Cross, I
don't know—and white pebbles and dark pebbles,
fishes, empty dories, yards of cable, coral, seaweed, and those are pearls that were his eyes. Like
that. You leave the thing alone, and after awhile it
takes it away again. That's how it operates. Oh
yeah—it also used to be lousy with condoms, limp,
almost transparent testimonies to the instinct to
continue the species but not tonight, and sometimes they were painted with snappy designs or
sayings and sometimes had a feather on the end.
These are almost gone now, I hear, the way of the
Edsel, the klepsydra and the button hook, shot
down and punctured by the safety pill, which makes
for larger mammaries, too, so who complains? Sometimes, as I'd walk along the beach in the sun-
spanked morning, the chill breezes helping me to
recover from the effects of rest and recuperation
leave from a small and neatly contained war in
Asia that had cost me a kid brother, sometimes
then I would hear the shrieking of birds when
there were no birds in sight. This added the ele-
ment of mystery that made the comparison inevi-
table: life is a thing that reminds me quite a bit of
the beaches around Tokyo Bay. Anything goes.
Strange and unique things are being washed up all
the time. I'm one of them and so are you. We
spend some time on the beach, maybe side by
side, and then that slopping, smelling, chilly thing
rakes it with the liquid fingers of a crumbling hand
and some of the things are gone again. The mysterious bird-cries are the open end of the human

condition. The voices of the gods? Maybe. Finally, to nail all corners of the comparison to the wall before we leave the room, there are two things that caused me to put it there in the first place: sometimes, I suppose, things that are taken away might, by some capricious current, be returned to the beach. I'd never seen it happen before, but maybe I hadn't waited around long enough. Also, you know, somebody could come along and pick up something he'd found there and take it away from the Bay. When I learned that the first of these two things might actually have happened, the first thing I did was puke. I'd been drinking and sniffing the fumes of an exotic plant for about three days. The next thing I did was expel all my house guests. Shock is a wonderful soberer, and I already knew that the second of the two things was possible—the taking away of a thing from the Bay—because it had happened to me, but I'd never figured on the first coming true. So I took a pill guaranteed to make me a whole man in three hours, followed it with a sauna bath and then stretched out on the big bed while the servants, mechanical and otherwise, took care of the cleaning up. Then I began to shake all over. I was scared.

I am a coward.

Now, there are a lot of things that scare me, and they are all of them things over which I have little or no control, like the Big Tree.

I propped myself up on my elbow, fetched the package from the bedside table and regarded its contents once more.

There could be no mistake, especially when a thing like that was addressed to me.

I had accepted the special delivery, stuffed it into my jacket pocket, opened it at my leisure.

Then I saw that it was the sixth, and I'd gotten sick and called things to a halt.

It was a tri-dee picture of Kathy, all in white, and it was dated as developed a month ago.

Kathy had been my first wife, maybe the only woman I'd ever loved, and she'd been dead for over five hundred years. I'll explain that last part by and by.

I studied the thing closely. The sixth such thing I'd received in as many months. Of different people, all of them dead. For ages.

Rocks and blue sky behind her, that's all.

It could have been taken anywhere where there were rocks and a blue sky. It could easily have been a fake, for there are people around who can fake almost anything these days.

But who was there around, now, who'd know enough to send it to me, and why? There was no note, just that picture, the same as with all the others—my friends, my enemies.

And the whole thing made me think of the beaches around Tokyo Bay, and maybe the Book of Revelations, too.

I drew a blanket over myself and lay there in the artificial twilight I had turned on at midday. I had been comfortable, so comfortable, all these years. Now something I had thought scabbed over, flaked away, scarred smoothly and forgotten had broken, and I bled.

If there was only the barest chance that I held a truth in my shaking hand . . .

I put it aside. After a time, I dozed, and I forget what thing out of sleep's mad rooms came to make me sweat so. Better forgotten, I'm sure.

I showered when I awoke, put on fresh clothing, ate quickly and took a carafe of coffee with me into my study. I used to call it an office when I worked, but around thirty-five years ago the habit wore off. I went through the past month's pruned and pre-sorted correspondence and found the items I was looking for amid the requests for money from some oddball charities and some oddball individuals who hinted at bombs if I didn't come across, four invitations to lecture, one to undertake what once might have been an interesting job, a load of periodicals, a letter from a long-lost descendant of an obnoxious in-law from my third marriage suggesting a visit, by him, with me, here, three solicitations from artists wanting a patron, thirty-one notices that lawsuits had been commenced against me and letters from various of my attorneys stating that thirty-one actions against me had been quashed.

The first of the important ones was a letter from Marling of Megapei. It said, roughly:

"Earth-son, I greet you by the twenty-seven Names that still remain, praying the while that you have cast more jewels into the darkness and given them to glow with the colors of life.

"I fear that the time of the life for the most ancient and dark green body I am privileged to wear moves now toward an ending early next year. It has been long since these yellow and failing eyes have seen my stranger son. Let it be before the ending of the fifth season that he comes to me, for all my cares will be with me then and his hand upon my shoulder would lighten their burden. Respects."

The next missive was from the Deep Shaft Mining and Processing Company, which everyone knows to be a front organization for Earth's Central Intelligence Department, asking me if I might be interested in purchasing some used-but-in-good-condition off-world mining equipment located at sites from which the cost of transport would be prohibitive to the present owners.

What it really said, in a code I'd been taught years before when I'd done a contract job for the federal government of Earth, was, *sans* officialese and roughly:

"What's the matter? Aren't you loyal to the home planet? We've been asking you for nearly twenty years to come to Earth and consult with us on a matter vital to planetary security. You have consistently ignored these requests. This is an urgent request and it requires your immediate cooperation on a matter of the gravest importance. We trust, and etc."

The third one said in English:

"I do not want it to seem as if I am trying to presume on something long gone by, but I am in serious trouble and you are the only person I can think of who might be able to help me. If you can possibly make it in the near future, please come see me on Aldebaran V. I'm still at the old address, although the place has changed quite a bit. Sincerely, Ruth."

Three appeals to the humanity of Francis Sandow. Which, if any of them, had anything to do with the pictures in my pocket?

The orgy I had called short had been a sort of going-away party. By now, all of my guests were on their ways off my world. When I had started it as an efficient means of getting them loaded and shipped away, I had known where *I* was going. The arrival of Kathy's picture, though, was making me think.

All three parties involved in the correspondence knew who Kathy had been. Ruth might once have had access to a picture of her, from which some talented person might work. Marling could have created the thing. Central Intelligence could have dug up old documents and had it forged in their labs. Or none of these. It was strange that there was no accompanying message, if somebody wanted something.

I had to honor Marling's request, or I'd never be able to live with myself. That had been first on my agenda, but now—I had through the fifth season, northern hemisphere, Megapei—which was still over a year away. So I could afford some other stops in between.

Which ones would they be?

Central Intelligence had no real claim on my services and Earth no dominion over me. While I was willing to help Earth if I could, the issue couldn't be so terribly vital if it had been around for the full twenty years they'd been pestering me. After all, the planet was still in existence, and according to the best information I had on the matter, was functioning as normally and poorly as usual. And for that matter, if I was as important to them as they made out in all their letters, *they* could have come and seen me.

But Ruth—

Ruth was another matter. We had lived together for almost a year before we'd realized we were cutting each other to ribbons and it just wasn't going to work out. We parted as friends, remained friends. She meant something to me. I was surprised she was still alive after all this time. But if she needed my help, it was hers.

So that was it. I'd go see Ruth, quickly, and try to bail her out of whatever jam she was in. Then I'd go to Megapei. And somewhere along the line, I might pick up a lead as to who, what, when, where, why and how I had received the pictures. If not, then I'd go to Earth and try Intelligence. Maybe a favor for a favor would be in order.

I drank my coffee and smoked. Then, for the first time in almost five years, I called my port and ordered the readying of the *Model T*, my jump-buggy, for the distance-hopping. It would take the rest of the day, much of the night, and be ready around sunrise, I figured.

Then I checked my automatic Secretary and Files to see who owned the *T* currently. S & F told me it was Lawrence J. Conner of Lochear— the "J" for "John." So I ordered the necessary identification papers, and they fell from the tube and into my padded in-basket about fifteen seconds later. I studied Conner's description, then called for my barber on wheels to turn my hair from dark brown to blond, lighten my suntan, toss on a few freckles, haze my eyes three shades darker and lay on some new fingerprints.

I have a whole roster of fictitious people, backgrounds complete and verifiable when you're away from their homes, people who have purchased the *T* from one another over the years, and others who will do so in the future. They are all of them around five feet, ten inches in height and weigh in at about one-sixty. They are all individuals I am capable of becoming with a bit of cosmetic and the memorization of a few facts. When I travel, I don't like the idea of doing it in a vessel registered in the name of Francis Sandow of Homefree or, as some refer to it, Sandow's World. While I'm quite willing to make the sacrifice and live with it, this is one of the drawbacks involved in being one of the hundred wealthiest men in the galaxy (I think I'm 87th, as of the last balance-sheet, but I could be 88th or 86th): somebody always wants something from you, and it's always blood or money, neither of which I am willing to spend too freely. I'm lazy and I scare easily and I just want to hang onto what I've got of both. If I had any sense of competition at all, I suppose I'd be busy trying to be 87th, 86th, or 85th, whichever. I don't care, though. I never did much, really, except maybe a little at first, and then the novelty quickly wore off. Anything over your first billion becomes metaphysical. I used to think of all the vicious things I was probably financing without realizing it. Then I came up with my Big Tree philosophy and decided the hell with the whole bit.

There is a Big Tree as old as human society, because that's what it is, and the sum total of its leaves, attached to all its branches and twigs, represents the amount of money that exists. There are names written on these leaves, and some fall off and new ones grow on, so that in a few seasons all the names have been changed. But the Tree stays pretty much the same: bigger, yes; and carrying on the same life functions as always, in pretty much the same way, too. I once went through a time when I tried to cut out all the rot I could find in the Tree. I found that as soon as I cut out a section in one place, it would occur somewhere else, and I had to sleep sometime. Hell, you can't even give money away properly these days; and the Tree is too big to bend like a *bonsai* in a bucket and so alter its growth. So I just let it grow on its merry way now, my name on all those leaves, some of them withered and sere and some bright with the first-green, and I try to enjoy myself, swinging around those branches and wearing a name that I don't see written all around me. So much for me and the Big Tree. The story of how I came to own so much greenery might provoke an even funnier, more elaborate and less botanical metaphor. If so, let's make it later. Too many, and look what happened to poor Johnny Donne: he started thinking he wasn't an Islande, and he's out there at the bottom of Tokyo Bay now and it doesn't diminish me one bit.

I began briefing S & F on everything my staff should do and not do in my absence. After many playbacks and much mindracking, I think I covered everything. I reviewed my last will and testament, saw nothing I wanted changed. I shifted certain papers to destruct-boxes and left orders that they be activated if this or that happened. I sent an alert to one of my representatives on Aldebaran

V, to let him know that if a man named Lawrence J-for-John Conner happened to pass that way and needed anything, it was his, and an emergency i.d. code, in case I had to be identified as me. Then I noticed that close to four hours had passed and I was hungry.

"How long to sunset, rounded to the nearest minute?" I asked S & F.

"Forty-three minutes," came its neuter-voiced reply through the hidden speaker.

"I will dine on the East Terrace in precisely thirty-three minutes," I said, checking my chronometer. "I will have a lobster with french fried potatoes and cole slaw, a basket of mixed rolls, a half-bottle of our own champagne, a pot of coffee, a lemon sherbert, the oldest Cognac in the cellar and two cigars. Ask Martin Bremen if he would do me the honor of serving it."

"Yes," said S & F. "No salad?"

"No salad."

Then I strolled back to my suite, threw a few things into a suitcase, and began changing clothes. I activated my bedroom hookup to S & F, and amidst a certain stomach-wringing, neck-chilling feeling, gave the order I had been putting off and could properly put off no longer:

"In exactly two hours and 11 minutes," I said, checking my chronometer, "ring Lisa and ask her if she would care to have a drink with me on the West Terrace—in half an hour's time. Prepare for her now two checks, each in the amount of fifty thousand dollars. Also, prepare for her a copy of Reference A. Deliver these items to this station, in separate, unsealed envelopes."

"Yes," came the reply, and while I was adjusting my cuff-links these items slid down the chute and came to rest in the basket on my dresser.

I checked the contents of the three envelopes, sealed them, placed them in an inside pocket of my jacket and made my way to the hallway that led to the East Terrace.

Outside, the sun, an amber giant now, was ambushed by a wispy strand which gave up in less than a minute and swam away. Hordes of overhead clouds wore gold, yellow and touches of deepening pink as the sun descended the merciless blue road that lay between Urim and Thumim, the twin peaks I had set just there to draw him and quarter him at each day's ending. His rainbow blood would splash their misty slopes during the final minutes.

I seated myself at my table beneath the elm tree. The overhead force-projector came on at the weight of my body upon the chair, keeping leaves, insects, bird droppings and dust from descending upon me from above. After a few moments, Martin Bremen approached, pushing a covered cart before him.

"Good efening, sir."

"Good evening, Martin. How go things with you?"

"Chust fine, Mister Sandow. And yourself?"

"I'm going away," I said.

"Ah?"

He laid the setting before me, uncovered the cart and began to serve the meal.

"Yes," I said, "maybe for quite some time."

I sampled my champagne and nodded approval.

". . . So I wanted to say something you're probably already aware of before I go. That is, you prepare the best meals I've ever eaten—"

"Thank you, Mister Sandow." His naturally ruddy face deepened a shade or two, and he fought the corners of his mouth into a straight line as he dropped his dark eyes. "I'fe enchoyed our association."

". . . So, if you'd care to take a year's vacation— full salary and all expenses, of course, plus a slush fund for buying any recipes you might be interested in trying—I'll call the Bursar's Office before I go, and set things up."

"Venn vill you be leafing, sir?"

"Early tomorrow morning."

"I see, sir. Yes. Thank you. That sounds wery pleasant."

". . . And find some more recipes for yourself while you're at it."

"I'll keep vun eye open, sir."

"It must be a funny feeling, preparing meals the taste of which you can't even guess at."

"Oh no, sir," he protested. "The tasters are completely reliable, and vile I'll admit I'fe often speculated as to the taste of some of your meals, the closest situation iss, I suppose, that of being a chemist who does not really vish to taste all of his experiments, if you know vatt I mean, sir."

He held the basket of rolls in one hand, the pot of coffee in his other hand, the dish of cole slaw in his other hand, and his other hand rested on the cart's handle. He was a Rigelian, whose name was something like Mmmrt'n Brrm'n. He'd learned his English from a German cook, who'd helped him

pick an English equivalent for Mmmrt'n Brrm'n.
A Rigelian chef, with a good taster or two from the
subject race, prepares the greatest meals in the
galaxy. They're quite dispassionate about it, too.
We'd been through the just-finished discussion
before, many times, and he knew I was always
kidding him when I talked that way, trying to get
him to admit that human food reminded him of
garbage, manure or industrial wastes. Apparently,
there is a professional ethic against acknowledging
any such thing. His normal counter is to be pain-
fully formal. On occasion, however, when he's had
a bit too much of lemon juice, orange juice or
grapefruit juice, he's as much as admitted that
cooking for *homo sapiens* is considered the lowest
level to which a Rigelian chef can stoop. I try to
make up to him for it as much as I can, because I
like him as well as his meals, and it's very hard to
get Rigelian chefs, no matter how much you can
afford to spend.

"Martin," I said, "if anything should happen to
me this time out, I'd like you to know that I've
made provision for you in my will."

"I—I don't know vatt to say, sir."

"So don't," I told him. "To be completely selfish
about it, I hope you don't collect. I plan on coming back."

He was one of the few persons to whom, with
impunity yet, I could mention such a thing. He
had been with me for thirty-two years and was
well past the point which would entitle him to a
good lifetime pension anyway. Preparing meals
was his dispassionate passion, though, and for some
unknown reason he seemed to like me. He'd make

out quite a bit better if I dropped dead that minute, but not enough to really make it worth his while to lace my cole slaw with Murtanian butterfly-venom.

"Look at that sunset, will you!" I decided.

He watched for a minute or two, then said, "You certainly do them up brown, sir."

"Thank you. You may leave the Cognac and cigars now and retire. I'll be here awhile."

He placed them on the table, drew himself up to his full eight feet of height, bowed, and said, "Best of luck on your churney, sir, and good efening."

"Sleep well," I said.

"Thank you," and he slithered away into the twilight.

When the cool night breezes slipped about me and the toadingales in their distant wallows began a Bach cantata, my orange moon Florida came up where the sun had gone down. The night-blooming danderoses spilled their perfumes upon the indigo air, the stars came on like aluminum confetti, the ruby-shrouded candle sputtered on my table, the lobster was warm and buttery in my mouth and the champagne cold as the heart of an iceberg. I felt a certain sadness and the desire to say "I will be back" to this moment of time.

So I finished the lobster, the champagne, the sherbert, and I lit a cigar before I poured a snifter of Cognac, which, I have been told, is a barbaric practice. I toasted everything in sight to make up for it, and then poured a cup of coffee.

When I had finished, I rose and took a walk around that big, complex building, my home. I moved up to the bar on the West Terrace and sat there with a Cognac in front of me. After a time, I lit my second cigar. Then she appeared in the archway, automatically falling into a perfume-ad pose.

Lisa wore a soft, silky blue thing that foamed about her in the light of the terrace, all sparkles and haze. She had on white gloves and a diamond choker; she was ash-blonde, the angles and curves of her pale-pink lips drawn up so that there was a circle between them, and she tilted her head far to one side, one eye closed, the other squinting.

"Well-met by moonlight," she said, and the circle broke into a smile, sudden and dewy, and I had timed it so that the second moon, pure white, was rising then in the west. Her voice reminded me of a recording stuck on a passage at middle C. They don't record things on discs that stick that way any more, but even if no one else remembers, I do.

"Hello," I said. "What are you drinking?"

"Scotch and soda," she said, as always. "Lovely night!"

I looked into her two too blue eyes and smiled. "Yes," as I punched out her order and the drink was made and delivered, "it is."

"You've changed. You're lighter."

"Yes."

"You're up to no good, I hope."

"Probably." I passed it to her. "It's been what?— Five months now?"

"A bit more."

"Your contract was for a year."

"That's right."

I passed her an envelope, and, "This cancels it," I said.

"What do you mean?" she asked, the smile freezing, diminishing, gone.

"Whatever I say, always," I said.

"You mean I'm dismissed?"

"I'm afraid so," I told her, "and here's a similar amount, to prove to you it isn't what you think." I passed her the second envelope.

"What is it, then?" she asked.

"I've got to go away. No sense to your wilting here in the meantime. I might be gone quite awhile."

"I'll wait."

"No."

"Then I'll go with you."

"Even if it means you might die along with me, if things go bad?"

I hoped she'd say yes. But after all this time I think I know something about people. That's why Reference A was handy.

"It's possible, this time around," I said. "Sometimes a guy like me has to take a few risks."

"Will you give me a reference?" she said.

"I have it here."

She sipped her drink.

"All right," she said.

I passed it to her.

"Do you hate me?" she asked.

"No."

"Why not?"

"Why?"

"Because I'm weak, and I value my life."

"So do I, though I can't guarantee it."

"That's why I'll accept the referral."

"That's why I have it ready."

"You think you know everything, don't you?"

"No."

"What will we do tonight?" she asked, finishing her drink.

"I don't know everything."

"Well, I know something. You've treated me all right."

"Thanks."

"I'd like to hang onto you."

"But I just scared you?"

"Yes."

"Too much?"

"Too much."

I finished my Cognac, puffed on the cigar, studied Florida and my white moon Cue Ball.

"Tonight," she said, taking my hand, "you'll at least forget to hate me."

She didn't open her envelopes. She sipped her second drink and regarded Florida and Cue Ball also.

"When will you leave?"

"Ere dawn," I said.

"God you're poetical."

"No, I'm just what I am."

"That's what I said."

"I don't think so, but it's been good knowing you."

She finished her drink and put it down.

"It's getting chilly out here."

"Yes."

"Let us repair within."

"I'd like to repair."

I put down my cigar and we stood and she kissed me. So I put my arm around her trim and sparkling, blue-kept waist and we moved away from the bar, toward the archway, through the archway and beyond, into the house we were leaving.

Let's make it a triple-asterisk break:

*   *   *

Perhaps the wealth I acquired along the way to becoming who I am is one of the things that made me one of the things that I am; *i.e.*, a bit of a paranoid. No.

It's too pat.

I could justify the qualms I feel each time I leave Homefree by saying that this is their source. Then I could turn around and justify that, by saying that it isn't really paranoia if there really are people out to get you. And there are, which is one of the reasons things are arranged to such an extent that I could stand all alone on Homefree and defy any man or government that wanted me to come and take me. They'd have to kill me, which would be a fairly expensive proposition, as it would entail destroying the entire planet. And even then, I think I've got an out that might work, though I've never had to test it under field conditions.

No, the real reason for my qualms is the very ordinary fear of death and non-being that all men know, intensified many times, though once I had a glimpse of a light that I can't explain . . . Forget that. There's me and maybe a few Sequoia trees that came onto the scene in the twentieth century and have managed to make it up until now, the thirty-second. Lacking the passivity of the plant kingdom, I learned after a time that the longer one exists the more strongly one becomes infected with a sense of mortality. Corollary to this, survival —once a thing I thought of primarily in Darwinian terms, as a pastime of the lower classes and phyla— threatens to become a preoccupation. It is a much subtler jungle now than it was in the days of my youth, with something like fifteen hundred inhabited worlds, each with its own ways of killing men, ways readily exportable when you can travel between the worlds in no time at all; seventeen other intelligent races, four of whom I consider smarter than men and seven or eight who are just as stupid, each with its own ways of killing men; multitudes of machines to serve us, numerous and ordinary as the automobile was when I was a kid, each with its own ways of killing men; new diseases, new weapons, new poisons and new mean animals, new objects of hatred, greed, lust and addiction, each with its own ways of killing men; and many, many, many new places to die. I've seen and met a lot of these things, and because of my somewhat unusual occupation there may be only twenty-six people in the galaxy who know more about them than I do.

So I'm scared, even though no one's shooting at me just now, the way they were a couple weeks before I got sent to Japan for rest and recuperation and found Tokyo Bay, say twelve hundred years ago. That's close. That's life.

*　　　*　　　*

I left in the dead of pre-dawn night without purposely saying goodbye to anybody, because that's the way I figure I have to be. I did wave back at a shadowy figure in the Operations Building who had waved at me after I'd parked my buggy and had begun walking across the field. But then, I was a shadowy figure, too. I reached the dock where the *Model T* sat squat, boarded her, stowed my gear, spent half an hour checking systems. Then I went outside to inspect the phase-projectors. I lit a cigarette.

In the east, the sky was yellow. A rumble of thunder came out of the dark mountains to the west. There were some clouds above me and the stars still clung to sky's faded cloak, less like confetti than dewdrops now.

For once, it wasn't going to happen, I decided.

Some birds sang, and a gray cat came and rubbed against my leg, then moved off in the direction of the birdsongs.

The breeze shifted so that it came up from the south, filtered through the forest that began at the far end of the field. It bore the morningdamp smells of life and growth.

The sky was pink as I took my last puff, and the mountains seemed to shiver within their shimmering as I turned and crushed it out. A large, blue bird floated toward me and landed on my shoulder. I stroked its plumage and sent it on its way.

I took a step toward the vehicle . . .

My toe struck a projecting bolt in a dock-plate and I stumbled. I caught hold of a strut and saved myself from a complete fall. I landed on one knee, and before I could get up a small, black bear was licking my face. I scratched his ears and patted his head, then slapped him on the rump as I rose. He turned and moved off toward the wood.

I tried to take another step, then realized that my sleeve was caught in the place where the strut I had grabbed crossed over another one.

By the time I'd disentangled myself, there was another bird upon my shoulder and a dark cloud of them flapping across the field from the direction of the forest. Above the noise of their cries, I heard more thunder.

It was happening.

I made a dash for the ship, almost stumbling over a green rabbit who sat on her haunches before the hatch, nose twitching, pink, myopic eyes staring in my direction. A big glass snake slithered toward me across the dock, transparent and gleaming.

I forgot to duck my head, banged it on the upper hatchplate and reeled back. My ankle was seized by a blonde monkey, who winked a blue eye at me.

So I patted her head and pulled free. She was stronger than she looked.

I passed through the hatch, and it jammed when I tried to close it.

By the time I'd worked it free, the purple parrots were calling my name and the snake was trying to come aboard.

I found a power-pull and used it.

"All right! Goddamn it!" I cried. "I'm going! Goodbye! I'll be back!"

The lightnings flashed and the thunders rolled and a storm began in the mountains and raced toward me. I worked the hatch free.

"Clear the field!" I yelled, and slammed it.

I dogged it shut, moved to the control seat and activated all systems.

On the screen, I saw the animals departing. Wisps of fog drifted by, and I heard the first drops of rain spattering on the hull.

I raised the ship, and the storm broke about me.

I got above it, left the atmosphere, accelerated, achieved orbit and set my course.

It's always like that when I try to leave Homefree, which is why I always try to sneak away without telling the place goodbye. It never works, though.

Anyway, it's nice to know that somewhere you are wanted.

*   *   *

At the proper moment, I broke orbit and raced away from the Homefree System. For several hours I was queasy and my hands tended to shake. I smoked too many cigarettes and my throat began to feel dry. Back at Homefree, I had been in charge of everything. Now, though, I was entering the big arena once again. For a moment, I actually contemplated turning back.

Then I thought of Kathy and Marling and Ruth and Nick the long dead dwarf and my brother Chuck, and I continued on to phase-point, hating myself.

It happened suddenly, just after I had entered phase and the ship was piloting itself.

I began laughing, and a feeling of recklessness came over me, just like in the old days.

What did it matter if I died? What was I living for that was so damned important? Eating fancy meals? Spending my nights with contract courtesans? Nuts! Sooner or later Tokyo Bay gets us all, and it would get me one day, too, I knew, despite everything. Better to be swept away in the pursuit of something halfway noble than to vegetate until someone finally figured a way to kill me in bed.

. . . And this, too, was a phase.

I began to chant a litany in a language older than mankind. It was the first time in many years that I had done so, for it was the first time in many years that I had felt fit to.

The light in the cabin seemed to grow dim, though I was sure it burnt as brightly as ever. The little dials on the console before me receded, became sparks, became the glowing eyes of animals peering at me from out of a dark wood. My voice now sounded like the voice of another, coming by some acoustical trick from a point far before me. Within myself, I followed it forward.

Then other voices joined in. Soon my own ceased, but the others continued, faint, high-pitched, fading and swelling as though borne by some unfelt wind; they touched lightly at my ears, not really beckoning. I couldn't make out any words, but they were singing. The eyes were all around me, neither advancing nor receding, and in the distance there was a very pale glow, as of sunset on a day filled with milk-clouds. I realized then that I was asleep and dreaming, and that I could awaken if I wished. I didn't, though. I moved on into the west.

At length, beneath a dream-pale sky, I came to

the edge of a cliff and could go no farther. There was water, water that I could not cross over, pale and sparkling, wraiths of mist folding and unfolding, slowly, above it; and out, far out from where I stood, one arm half-extended, crag piled upon terrace upon cold terrace, rocky buttresses all about, fog-dimmed pinnacles indicating a sky that I could not see, the whole stark as a sandblasted iceberg of ebony, I beheld the source of the singing, and a chillness clutched at my neck and perhaps the hair rose upon it.

I saw the shades of the dead, drifting like the mists or standing, half-hid, by the dark rocks of that place. And I knew that they were the dead, for among them I saw Nick the dwarf, gesturing obscenely, and I saw the telepath Mike Shandon, who had almost toppled an empire, *my* empire, the man I had slain with my own hands, and there was my old enemy Dango the Knife, and Courtcour Bodgis, the man with the computer mind, and Lady Karle of Algol, whom I had loved and hated.

Then I called upon that which I hoped I could still call upon.

There came a rumble of thunder and the sky grew as bright and blue as a pool of azure mercury. I saw her standing there for a moment, out across those waters in that dark place, Kathy, all in white, and our eyes met and her mouth opened and I heard my name spoken but nothing more, for the next clap of thunder brought with it total darkness and laid it upon that isle and the one who had stood upon the cliff, one arm half-extended. Me, I guess.

*   *   *

When I awoke, I had a rough idea of what it had meant. A rough idea only. And I couldn't understand it worth a damn, though I tried to analyze it.

I had once created Boecklin's Isle of the Dead to satisfy the whim of a board of unseen clients, strains of Rachmaninoff dancing like phantom sugar plums through my head. It had been a rough piece of work. Especially, since I am a creature who thinks in a mostly pictorial format. Whenever I think of death, which is often, there are two pictures that take turns filling my mind. One is the Valley of Shadows, a big, dark valley beginning between two massive prows of gray stone, with a greensward that starts out twilit and just gets darker and darker as you stare farther and farther into it, until finally you are staring into the blackness of interstellar space itself, *sans* stars, comets, meteors, anything; and the other is that mad painting by Boecklin, *The Isle of the Dead*, of the place I had just viewed in the land of dream. Of the two places, the Isle of the Dead is far more sinister. The Valley seems to hold a certain promise of peace. This, however, may be because I never designed and built a Valley of Shadows, sweating over every nuance and overtone of that emotion-wringing landscape. But in the midst of an otherwise Eden, I had raised up an Isle of the Dead one time, and it had burnt itself into my consciousness to such an extent that not only could I never wholly forget it, but I had become a part of it as surely as it was a part of me. Now, this part of myself had just addressed me in the only way that it could, in response to a sort of prayer. It was warning me, I felt, and it was also giving me a clue, a clue that might make sense as time went on. Symbols, by their very nature, conceal as well as indicate, damn them!

Kathy *had* seen me, within the fabric of my vision, which meant that there might be a chance . . .

I turned on the screen and regarded the spirals of light, moving in both clockwise and counterclockwise directions about a point directly before me. These were the stars, visible only in this fashion, there, on the underside of space. As I hung there and the universe moved about me, I felt the decades' layers of fat that padded my soul's midsection catch fire and begin to burn. The man I had worked so hard at becoming died then, I hope, and I felt that Shimbo of Darktree Tower, Shrugger of Thunders, still lived.

I watched the spinning stars, grateful, sad and proud, as only a man who has outlived his destiny and realized he might yet forge himself another, can be.

After a time, the whirlpool in the sky sucked me down to sleep's dark center, dreamless and cool, soft and still, like the Valley of Shadows perhaps.

*   *   *

It was as two weeks' time before Lawrence Conner brought his *Model T* to berth on Aldebaran V, which is called Driscoll, after its discoverer. It was as two weeks inside the *Model T*, though no time at all passed during phase. Don't ask me why, please. I don't have time to write a book. But had Lawrence Conner decided to turn around and head back for Homefree, he could have enjoyed another two weeks of calisthenics, introspection and reading and quite possibly have made it back on the afternoon of the same day Francis Sandow had departed, doubtless pleasing the wildlife no end. He didn't, though. Instead, he helped Sandow nail down a piece of the briar business, which he didn't really want, just to keep up appearances while he examined the puzzle-pieces he'd found. Maybe they were pieces from several different puzzles, all mixed together. There was no way of telling.

I wore a light tropical suit and sunglasses, for the yellow sky had in it only a few orange-colored clouds and the sun beat waves of heat about me, and they broke upon the pastel pavements where they splashed and rose in a warm, reality-distorting spray. I drove my rented vehicle, a slip-sled, into the art colony of a city called Midi, a place too sharp and fragile and necessarily beside the sea for my liking—with nearly all its towers, spires, cubes and ovoids that people call home, office, studio, or shop built out of that stuff called glacyllin, which may be made transparent in a colorless or tinted fashion and opaqued at any color, by means of a simple, molecule-disturbing control—and I sought out Nuage, a street down by the waterfront, driving through a town that constantly changed color about me, reminding me of molded jello—raspberry, strawberry, cherry, orange, lemon and lime—with lots of fruits inside.

I found the place, at the old address, and Ruth had been right.

It had changed, quite a bit. It had been one of the few strongholds against the creeping jello that ate the city, back when we had lived there together. Now it, too, had succumbed. Where once there had been a high, stucco wall enclosing a cobbled courtyard, a black iron gate set within its archway, a hacienda within, sprawled about a small pool where the waters splashed sun-ghosts on the rough walls and the tiles, now there was a castle of jello with four high towers. Raspberry, yet.

I parked, crossed a rainbow bridge, touched the announcement-plate on the door.

"This home is vacant," reported a mechanical voice through a concealed speaker.

"When will Miss Laris be back?" I asked.

"This home is vacant," it repeated. "If you are interested in purchasing it, you may contact Paul Glidden at Sunspray Realty, Incorporated, 178 Avenue of the Seven Sighs."

"Did Miss Laris leave a forwarding address?"

"No."

"Did she leave any messages?"

"No."

I returned to the slip-sled, raised it onto an eight-inch cushion of air and sought out the Avenue of the Seven Sighs, which had once been called Main Street.

He was fat and lacking in hair, except for a pair of gray eyebrows about two inches apart, each thin enough to have been drawn on with a single pencil-stroke, high up there over eyes slate-gray and serious, higher still above the pink catenary mouth that probably even smiled when he slept, there, under the small, upturned thing he breathed through, which looked even smaller and more turned-up because of the dollops of dough his cheeks that threatened to rise even further and engulf it completely, along with all the rest of his features, leaving him a smooth, suffocating lump (save for the tiny, pierced ears with the sapphires in them), turning as ruddy as the wide-sleeved shirt that covered his northern hemisphere, Mister Glidden, behind his desk at Sunspray, lowering the moist hand I had just shaken, his Masonic ring clicking against the ceramic sunburst of his ashtray as he picked up his cigar, in order to study me, fish-like, from the lake of smoke into which he submerged.

"Have a seat, Mister Conner," he chewed. "What have I got that you want?"

"You're handling Ruth Laris' place, over on Nuage, aren't you?"

"That's right. Think you might want to buy it?"

"I'm looking for Ruth Laris," I said. "Do you know where she's moved?"

A certain luster went out of his eye.

"No," he said. "I've never met Ruth Laris."

"She must want you to send the money someplace."

"That's right."

"Mind telling me where?"

"Why should I?"

"Why not? I'm trying to locate her."

"I'm to deposit in her account at a bank."

"Here in town?"

"That is correct. Artists Trust."

"But she didn't make the arrangements with you?"

"No. Her attorney did."

"Mind telling me who he is?"

He shrugged, down there in his pool. "Why not?" he said. "Andre DuBois, at Benson, Carling and Wu. Eight blocks north of here."

"Thanks."

"You're not interested in the property then, I take it?"

"On the contrary," I said. "I'll buy the place, if I can take possession this afternoon—and if I can discuss the deal with her attorney. How does fifty-two thousand sound?"

Suddenly he was out of his pool.

"Where may I call you, Mister Conner?"

"I'll be staying at the Spectrum."

"After five?"

"After five is fine."

So what to do?

First, I checked in at the Spectrum. Second, using the proper code, I contacted my man on Driscoll to arrange for the necessary quantity of cash to be available to Lawrence Conner for the purchase. Third, I drove down to the religious district, parked the sled, got out, began walking.

I walked past shrines and temples dedicated to Everybody, from Zoroaster to Jesus Christ. I slowed when I came to the Pei'an section.

After a time, I found it. All there was above the ground was an entranceway, a green place about the size of a one-car garage.

I passed within and descended a narrow stairway.

I reached a small, candle-lit foyer and moved on through a low arch.

I entered a dark shrine containing a central altar decked out in a deep green, tiers of pews all about it.

There were hundreds of stained glassite plates on all five walls, depicting the Pei'an deities. Maybe I shouldn't have gone there that day. It had been so long . . .

There were six Pei'ans and eight humans present, and four of the Pei'ans were women. They all wore prayer-straps.

Pei'ans are about seven feet tall and green as grass. Their heads look like funnels, flat on top, their necks like the necks of funnels. Their eyes are enormous and liquid green or yellow. Their noses are flat upon their faces—wrinkles parenthesizing nostrils the size of quarters. They have no hair whatsoever. Their mouths are wide and they don't really have any teeth in them, per se. Like, I guess the best example is an elasmobranch. They are constantly swallowing their skins. They lack lips, but their dermis bunches and hardens once it goes internal and gives them horny ridges with which to chew. After that, they digest it, as it moves on and is replaced by fresh matter. However this may sound to someone who has never met a Pei'an, they are lovely to look at, more graceful than cats, older than mankind, and wise, very. Other than this, they are bilaterally symmetrical and possess two arms and two legs, five digits per. Both sexes wear jackets and skirts and sandals, generally dark in color. The women are shorter, thinner, larger about the hips and chests than the men—although the women have no breasts, for their young do not nurse, but digest great layers of fat for the first several weeks of their lives, and then begin to digest their skins. After a time, they eat food, pulpy mashes and seastuff mainly. That's Pei'ans.

Their language is difficult. I speak it. Their philosophies are complex. I know some of them. Many of them are telepaths, and some have other unusual abilities. Me, too.

I seated myself in a pew and relaxed. I draw a certain psychic strength from Pei'an shrines, because of my conditioning in Megapei. The Pei'ans are exceedingly polytheistic. Their religion reminds me a bit of Hinduism, because they've never discarded anything—and it seems they spent their entire history accumulating deities, rituals, traditions. Strantri is what the religion is called, and over the years it has spread considerably. It stands a good chance of becoming a universal religion one day because there's something in it to satisfy just about anybody, from animists and pantheists through agnostics and people who just like rituals. Native Pei'ans only constitute around ten percent of the Strantrians now, and theirs will probably be the first large-scale religion to outlive its founding race. There are fewer Pei'ans every year. As individuals, they have godawful long lifespans, but they're not very fertile. Since their greatest scholars have already written the last chapter in the immense *History of Pei'an Culture*, in 14,926 volumes, they may have decided that there's no reason to continue things any further. They have an awful lot of respect for their scholars. They're funny that way.

They had a galactic empire back when men were still living in caves. Then they fought an ages-long war with a race which no longer exists, the Bahulians—which sapped their energies, racked their industries and decimated their number. Then they gave up their outposts and gradually withdrew to the small system of worlds they inhabit today. Their home world—also called Megapei— had been destroyed by the Bahulians, who by all accounts were ugly, ruthless, vicious, fierce and depraved. Of course, all these accounts were written by the Pei'ans, so I guess we'll never know what the Bahulians were really like. They weren't Strantrians, though, because I read somewhere that they were idolators.

On the side of the shrine opposite the archway, one of the men began chanting a litany that I recognized better than any of the others, and I looked up suddenly to see if it had happened.

It had.

The glassite plate depicting Shimbo of Darktree, Shrugger of Thunders, was glowing now, green and yellow.

Some of their deities are Pei'apomorphic, to coin a term, while others, like the Egyptians', look like crosses between Pei'ans and things you might find in a zoo. Still others are just weird-looking. And somewhere along the line, I'm sure they must have visited the Earth, because Shimbo is a man. Why any intelligent race would care to make a god of a savage is beyond me, but there he stands, naked, with a slight greenish cast to his complexion, his face partly hidden by his upraised left arm, which holds a thunder cloud in the midst of a yellow sky. He bears a great bow in his right hand and a quiver of thunderbolts hangs at his hip. Soon all six Pei'ans and the eight humans were chanting the same litany. More began to file in through the door. The place began to fill up.

A great feeling of light and power began in my middle section and expanded to fill my entire body.

I don't understand what makes it happen, but whenever I enter a Pei'an shrine, Shimbo begins to glow like that, and the power and the ecstasy is always there. When I completed my thirty-year course of training and my twenty-year apprenticeship in the trade that made me my fortune, I was the only Earthman in the business. The other worldscapers are all Pei'ans. Each of us bears a Name—one of the Pei'an deities'—and this aids us in our work, in a complex and unique fashion. I chose Shimbo—or he chose me—because he seemed to be a man. For so long as I live, it is believed that he will be manifest in the physical universe. When I die, he returns to the happy nothing, until another may bear the Name. Whenever a Name-bearer enters a Pei'an shrine, that deity is illuminated in his place—in every shrine in the galaxy. I do not understand the bond. Even the Pei'ans don't, really.

I had thought that Shimbo had long since forsaken me, because of what I had done with the Power and with my life. I had come to this shrine, I guess, to see if it was true.

I rose and made my way to the archway. As I passed through it, I felt an uncontrollable desire to raise my left hand. Then I clenched my fist and drew it back down to shoulder level. As I did, there came a peal of thunder from almost directly overhead.

Shimbo still shone upon the wall and the chanting filled my head as I walked up the stairway and out into the world where a light rain had begun to fall.

II

GLIDDEN AND I met in DuBois' office at 6:30 and concluded the deal, for fifty-six thousand. DuBois was a short man with a weatherbeaten face and a long shock of white hair. He'd opened his office at that hour because of my insistence on dealing that afternoon. I paid the money, the papers were signed, the keys were in my pocket, hands were shaken all around and the three of us departed. As we walked across the damp pavement toward our respective vehicles, I said, "Damn! I left my pen on your desk, DuBois!"

"I'll have it sent to you. You're staying at the Spectrum?"

"I'm afraid I'll be checking out very shortly."

"I can send it to the place on Nuage."

I shook my head. "I'll be needing it tonight."

"Here. Take this one." He offered me his own.

By then Glidden had entered his vehicle and was out of earshot. I waved to him, then said,

"That was for his benefit. I want to speak with you in private."

The squint that suddenly surrounded his dark eyes removed their look of incipient disgust and replaced it with one of curiosity.

"All right," he said, and we re-entered the building and he unlocked his office door again.

"What is it?" he asked, reassuming the padded chair behind his desk.

"I'm looking for Ruth Laris," I said.

He lit a cigarette, which is always a good way to buy a little thinking time.

"Why?" he asked.

"She's an old friend. Do you know where she is?"

"No," he said.

"Isn't it a trifle—unusual—to conserve assets in this quantity for a person whose whereabouts you don't even know?"

"Yes," he said, "I'd say so. But that is what I've been retained to do."

"By Ruth Laris?"

"What do you mean by that?"

"Did she retain you personally, or did somebody else do it on her behalf?"

"I don't see that this is any business of yours, Mister Conner. I believe I am going to call this conversation to a close."

I thought a second, made a quick decision.

"Before you do," I said, "I want you to know that I bought her house only to search it for clues as to her whereabouts. After that, I'm going to indulge a whim and convert it into a hacienda, because I don't like the architecture in this city. What does that indicate to you?"

"That you're something of a nut," he observed.

I nodded and added, "A nut who can afford to indulge his whims. Therefore a crackpot who can cause a lot of trouble. What's *this* building worth? A couple million?"

"I don't know." He looked a little uneasy.

"What if someone bought it for an apartment building and you had to go looking for another office?"

"My lease would not be that easy to cancel, Mister Conner."

I chuckled. ". . . And then," I said, "you were suddenly to find yourself the subject of an inquiry by the local Bar Association?"

He sprang to his feet.

"You *are* a madman."

"Are you sure? I don't know what the charges would be," I said, "yet. But you know that even an inquiry would give you some trouble—and then if you started running into difficulties finding another place . . ." I didn't like doing things this way, but I was in a hurry. So, "Are you sure? Are you very sure that I'm a madman?" I finished.

Then, "No," he said, "I'm not."

"Then, if you've nothing to hide, why not tell me how the arrangements were made? I'm not interested in the substance of any privileged communications, simply the circumstances surrounding the house's being put up for sale. It puzzles me that Ruth didn't leave a message of any sort."

He leaned his head against the back of his chair and studied me through smoke.

"The arrangements were made by phone—"

"She could have been drugged, threatened . . ."

"That is ridiculous," he said. "What is your interest in this, anyway?"

"Like I said, she's an old friend."

His eyes widened and then narrowed. A few people still knew who one of Ruth's old friends had been.

". . . Also," I continued, "I received a message from her recently, asking me to come see her on a matter of some urgency. She is not here and there is no message, no forwarding address. It smells funny. I am going to find her, Mister DuBois."

He was not blind to the cut and therefore the cost of my suit, and maybe my voice has a somewhat authoritarian edge from years of giving orders. At any rate, he didn't switch on the phone and call for the cops.

"All the arrangements were made over the phone and through the mails," he said. "I honestly do not know where she is presently. She simply said that she was leaving town and wanted me to dispose of the place and everything in it, the money to be deposited in her account at Artists Trust. So I agreed to handle the matter and turned it over to Sunspray." He looked away, looked back. "Now, she did leave a message with me, to be delivered to someone other than yourself should he call here for it. If not, I am to transmit it to that individual after thirty days have elapsed from the time I received it."

"May I inquire as to the identity of that individual?"

"That, sir, *is* privileged."

"Switch on the phone," I said, "and call 73737373

in Glencoe, reversing the charges. Make it person-to-person to Domenic Malisti, the director of Our Thing Enterprises on this planet. Identify yourself, say to him, 'Baa baa blacksheep' and ask him to identify Lawrence John Conner for you."

DuBois did this, and when he hung up he rose to his feet, crossed the office, opened a small wall safe, removed an envelope and handed it to me. It was sealed, and across the face of it lay the name "Francis Sandow," typewritten.

"Thank you," I said and tore it open.

I fought down my feelings as I regarded the three items the envelope contained. There was another picture of Kathy, different pose, slightly different background, a picture of Ruth, older and a bit heavier but still attractive, and a note.

The note was written in Pei'an. Its salutation named me and was followed by a small sign which is used in holy texts to designate Shimbo, Shrugger of Thunders. It was signed "Green Green," and followed by the ideogram for Belion, who was not one of the twenty-seven Names which lived.

I was perplexed. Very few know the identities of the Name-bearers, and Belion is the traditional enemy of Shimbo. He is the fire god who lives under the earth. He and Shimbo take turns hacking one another up between resurrections.

I read the note. It said, *If you want your women, seek them on the Isle of the Dead. Bodgis, Dango, Shandon and the dwarf are also waiting.*

Back on Homefree there were tri-dees of Bodgis, Dango, Shandon, Nick, Lady Karle (who might qualify as one of my women) and Kathy. Those were the six pictures I'd received. Now he'd taken Ruth.

Who?

I did not know Green Green from anywhere that I could recall, but of course I knew the Isle of the Dead.

"Thank you," I said again.

"Is something wrong, Mister Sandow?"

"Yes," I said, "but I'll set it right. Don't worry, you're not involved. Forget my name."

"Yes, Mister Conner."

"Good evening."

"Good evening."

*   *   *

I entered the place on Nuage. I walked through the foyer, the various living rooms. I found her bedroom and searched it. She had left the place completely furnished. She'd also left several closets and dressers full of clothing, and all sorts of little personal items that you just don't leave behind when you move. It was a funny feeling, walking through that place which had replaced the other place and every now and then seeing something familiar—an antique clock, a painted screen, an inlaid cigarette box—reminding me how life redistributes what once was meaningful amidst the always to be foreign, killing its personal magic, save in a memory you carry of the time and the place where once it stood, until you meet it again, it troubles you briefly, surrealistically, and then that magic, too, dies away as, punctured by the encounter, emotions you had forgotten are drained from the pictures inside your head. At least, it happened to me that way, as I searched for clues as to what might have occurred. As the hours passed and, one by one, each item in the place was passed through the sieve of my scrutiny, the realization which had come upon me in DuBois' office, the thing that had ridden with me from Homefree since the day the first picture had arrived, completed its circuit: brain to intestines to brain.

I seated myself and lit a cigarette. This was the room where the photo of Ruth had been taken; hers hadn't been the rocks-and-blue-sky setting of the others. I had searched though and found nothing: no evidence of violence, no clue as to the identity of my enemy. I said the words aloud, "My enemy," the first words I had spoken since "Good evening" to the suddenly cooperative, white-haired attorney, and the words sounded strange in that big fishbowl of a place. My enemy.

It was out in the open now. I was wanted, for what I wasn't sure. Offhand, I'd say death. It would have been helpful if I could have known which of my many enemies was behind it. I searched my mind. I considered my enemy's odd choice of rendezvous-point, battlefield. I thought back upon my dream of the place.

It was a foolish place for anyone to lure me if he wished to harm me, unless he knew nothing whatsoever concerning my power once I set foot upon any world I've made. Everything would be my ally if I went back to Illyria, the world I'd put where it was, many centuries ago, the world which held the Isle of the Dead, *my* Isle of the Dead.

. . . And I would go back. I knew that. Ruth, and the possibility of Kathy . . . These required my return to that strange Eden I'd once laid out. Ruth and Kathy . . . Two images which I did not like to juxtapose, but had to. They had never existed simultaneously for me, and I did not like the feeling now. I'd go, and whoever had baited the trap in this fashion would be sorry for a brief time only, and then he would dwell upon the Isle of the Dead forever.

I crushed out my cigarette, locked the ruddy castle gate and drove back to the Spectrum. I was suddenly hungry.

I dressed for dinner and descended to the lobby. I'd noticed a decent-looking little restaurant off to the left. Unfortunately, it had just closed a few minutes before. So I inquired at the desk after a good eating place that was still open.

"Bartol Towers, on the Bay," said the night clerk, smothering a yawn. "They'll be open for several hours yet."

So I took his directions on how to get there, and went out and nailed down a piece of the briar business. Ridiculous is a better word than strange, but then everybody lives in the shade of the Big Tree, remember?

I drove over, and I left the slip-sled to be parked by a uniform which I see wherever I go, smiling face above it, opening before me doors which I can open for myself, handing me a towel I don't want, snatching at a briefcase I don't care to check, right hand held at waist-level and ready to turn palm up at the first glint of metal or the crinkling of the proper type paper, large pockets to hold these items. It has followed me for over a thousand years, and it's not really the uniform that I resent. It's that damned smile, which is turned on by one thing only. My car went from here to there and was dropped between a pair of painted lines. Because we are all tourists.

At one time, tips were given only for things you logically would want to have done efficiently and promptly, and they served to supplement a lower payscale for certain classes of employment. This was understood, accepted. It was tourism, back in the century of my birth, cluing in the underdeveloped countries to the fact that all tourists are marks, that set the precedent, which then spread to all countries, even back to the tourists' own, of the benefits which might be gained by those who wear uniforms and render the undesired and the unrequested with a smile. This is the army that conquered the world. After their quiet revolution in the twentieth century, we all became tourists the minute we set foot outside our front doors, second-class citizens, to be ruthlessly exploited by the smiling legions who had taken over, slyly, completely.

Now, in every city into which I venture, uniforms rush upon me, dust dandruff from my collar, press a brochure into my hand, recite the latest weather report, pray for my soul, throw walkshields over nearby puddles, wipe off my windshield, hold an umbrella over my head on sunny or rainy days, or shine an ultra-infra flashlight before me on cloudy ones, pick lint from my bellybutton, scrub my back, shave my neck, zip up my fly, shine my shoes and smile—all before I can protest—right hand held at waist-level. What a goddamn happy place the universe would be if everyone wore uniforms that glinted and crinkled. Then we'd all have to smile at each other.

I took the elevator up to the sixtieth floor, where the big place was. Then I realized that I should have called ahead from the hotel for a reservation. It was crowded. I'd forgotten that the following day was a holiday on Driscoll. The hostess took my name and told me fifteen or twenty minutes, so I went into one of a pair of bars and ordered a beer.

I looked about me as I sipped, and across the little foyer in the matching bar on the other side, hovering in the gloom, I saw a fat face that looked somewhat familiar. I slipped on a pair of special glasses which act like telescopes, and I studied the face, now in profile. The nose and the ears were the same. The hair was the wrong color and the complexion darker, but that's easily done.

I got up and started to walk that way when a waiter stopped me and told me that I couldn't carry a drink out of the place. When I told him I was going to the other bar, he offered to carry the drink for me, smiling, right hand at waist-level. I figured it would be cheaper to buy another one, so I told him he could drink it for me, too.

He was alone, a tiny glass of something bright before him. I folded my glasses and tucked them away as I approached his table, and in a fake-falsetto said, "May I join you, Mister Bayner?"

He jumped, just slightly, within his skin, and the fat only quivered for an instant. He photographed me with his magpie eyes in the following second, and I knew that the machine that lay behind them was already spinning its wheels like a demon on an exercise bike.

"You must be mistaken—" he began, and smiled then, and followed that with a frown. "No, *I* am," he corrected himself, "but then it's been a long time, Frank, and we've both changed."

". . . Into our traveling clothes, yes," I said in my normal voice, seating myself across from him.

He caught the attention of a waiter as easily as if he'd had a lariat, and he asked me, "What are you drinking?"

"Beer," I said, "any brand."

The waiter overheard me, nodded, departed.

"Have you eaten?"

"No, I was waiting for a table, across the way there, when I spotted you."

"I've already eaten," he said. "If I hadn't indulged a sudden desire for an after-dinner drink on my way out, I might have missed you."

"Strange," I said, then, "Green Green."

"What?"

"*Verde Verde. Grün. Grün.*"

"I'm afraid I don't follow you. Is that some kind of code-phrase I'm supposed to recognize?"

I shrugged.

"Call it a prayer for the confoundment of my enemies. What's new?"

"Now that you're here," he said, "I've got to talk with you, of course. May I join you?"

"Surely."

So, when they called for Larry Conner, we moved to a table in one of the countless dining rooms that filled that floor of the tower. We'd have had a pleasant view of the bay on a clear night, but the sky was overcast and an occasional buoy-light and an unpleasantly rapid searchlight were all that shone above the dark swells of the ocean. Bayner decided that he had a bit of an appetite left and ordered a full meal. He shoveled away a mound of spaghetti and a mess of bloody looking sausages before I'd half-finished my steak, and he moved on to shortcake, cheesecake and coffee.

"Ah, that was good!" he said, and he immediately inserted a toothpick into the upper portion of the first smile I'd seen him smile in, say, forty years.

"Cigar?" I offered.

"Thank you, I believe I will."

The toothpick went away, the cigars were lit, the check arrived. I always do that in crowded places when they're slow to bring me the check. A lit stogie, a quick blue haze and they're right beside me with the tab.

"This is on me," he announced as I accepted the bill.

"Nonsense. You're my guest."

"Well . . . All right."

After all, Bill Bayner is the forty-fifth wealthiest man in the galaxy. It isn't every day I get a chance to dine with successful people.

As we left, he said, "I've got a place where we can talk. I'll drive."

So we took his car, leaving a uniform and a frown behind us, and spent about twenty minutes driving around the city, shaking off hypothetical tails, and we finally arrived at an apartment building about eight blocks from Bartol Towers. As we entered the lobby, he nodded to the doorman, who nodded back to him.

"Think it'll rain tomorrow?" he asked.

"Clear," said the doorman.

Then we rode up to the sixth floor. The wainscotting in the hallway was full of artificial gems, some of which had to be eyes. We stopped and he knocked at an ordinary-looking door: three, pause, two, pause, two. He'd change it tomorrow, I knew. A dour-faced young man in a dark suit answered the door, nodded, and departed when Bayner gestured over his shoulder with a thumb. Inside, he secured the door, but not before I'd noticed from its edge that a metal plate was sandwiched between its inner and outer veneers of fake wood. For the next five or ten minutes, he tested the room with an amazing variety of bug-detection equipment, after giving me a keep-quiet sign, and then set several bug-scramblers into operation as an added precaution, sighed, removed his jacket and hung it on the back of a chair, turned to me and said, "It's okay to talk now. Can I fix you a drink?"

"Are you sure it'll be safe?"

He thought about it for a moment, then said, "Yes."

"Then I'll have bourbon and water if you've got it."

He withdrew into the next room and returned after about a minute with two glasses. His was probably filled with tea if he was planning on talking any kind of business with me. I couldn't have cared less.

"So what's up?" I asked him.

"Damn it, the stories they tell about you are true, aren't they? How'd you find out?"

I shrugged.

"But you're not going to move in on me on this one, not the way you did on those Vegan mining franchises."

"I don't know what you're talking about," I said.

"Six years ago."

I laughed.

"Listen," I told him, "I don't pay much attention to what my money does, so long as it's there when I want it. I trust various people to handle it for me. If I got a good deal in the Vegan system six years ago, it's because some good man in my employ lined it up. I don't run around shepherding money the way you do. I've delegated all that."

"Sure, sure, Frank," he said. "So you're incognito on Driscoll and you arrange to run into me the night before I deal. Who'd you buy on my staff?"

"Nobody, believe me."

He looked hurt.

"I'd tell *you*," he said. "I won't hurt him. I'll just transfer him somewhere where he won't do any more harm."

"I'm really not here on business," I said, "and I ran into you by pure chance."

"Well, you're not going to grab the whole thing this time, whatever you've got up your sleeve," he said.

"I'm not even in the running. Honest."

"Damn it!" he said. "Everything was going so smoothly!" and his right fist smashed against his left palm.

"I haven't even seen the product," I said.

He got up and stalked out of the room, came back and handed me a pipe.

"Nice pipe," I said.

"Five thousand," he told me. "Cheap."

"I'm really not much of a pipe-smoker."

"I won't cut you in for more than ten percent," he said. "I've been handling this thing personally, and you're not going to queer it."

And then I got mad. All that bastard thought about, besides eating, was stacking up his wealth. He automatically assumed I spent my time the same way, just because a lot of leaves on the Big Tree say "Sandow." So, "I want a third, or I make my own deal," I said.

"A third?"

He leaped to his feet and began screaming. It was a good thing that the room was soundproof and debugged. It had been a long time since I'd heard some of those expressions. He grew red in the face and he paced. Greedy, money-grubbing, unethical me sat there thinking about pipes while he ranted.

A guy with a memory like mine has many odd facts in his head. Back in my youth, on Earth, the best pipes were made either of meerschaum or briar. Clay pipes draw awfully hot and wooden ones crack or burn out quickly. Corncobs are dangerous. In the latter part of the twentieth century, possibly because of a generation growing up in the shadow of a Surgeon General's Report on respiratory diseases, pipe smoking had undergone something of a renaissance. By the turn of the century, the world's supply of briar and meerschaum was largely exhausted. Meerschaum, or hydrous magnesium silicate, is a sedimentary rock which occurred in strata composed in part of seashells that had fused together over the ages, and when it was all gone, that was it. Briar pipes were made from the root of the White Heath, or *Erica Arborea,* which grew only in a few areas about the Mediterranean and had to be around a hundred years old before it was of any use. The White Heath had been subjected to wanton harvesting, with anything like a reforestation plan far from mind. Consequently, substances like pyrolitic carbon now do for the bulk of pipe smokers, but meerschaum and briar linger in memories and collections. Small deposits of meerschaum have been discovered upon various worlds and turned into fortunes overnight. Nowhere but on Earth, however, has *Erica Arborea* or a suitable substitute ever turned up. And pipe smoking is the mainliner's way of smoking these days, DuBois and me being mavericks. The pipe Bayner had shown me was a pretty, flame-grained briar. Therefore . . .

". . . Fifteen percent," he was saying, "which barely allows me a small profit—"

"Nuts! Those briars are worth ten times their weight in platinum!"

"You cut my heart out if you ask for more than eighteen percent!"

"Thirty."

"Be reasonable, Frank."

"Then let's talk business, not nonsense."

"Twenty percent is all I can let you in for, and it will cost you five million—"

I laughed.

So for the next hour I haggled, out of pure cussedness, resenting the estimation he'd placed on me and refused to disbelieve. I lived up to it, too. Like twenty-five and a half percent for four million, which required a phone call to Malisti to swing the financing. I really hated to wake him.

And that's how I nailed down a piece of the briar business on Driscoll. Ridiculous is a better word than strange, but then everyone lives in the shade of the Big Tree, remember?

After it was all over, he slapped me on the shoulder and told me I was a cool dealer and that he'd rather have me with him than against him, made us another round of drinks, sounded me out on getting Martin Bremen away from me, as he'd never been able to hire a Rigelian chef, and asked me once again who had tipped me off.

He dropped me at Bartol Towers, the uniform moved my car a few feet and held the door for me, got its money, turned off its smile and went away. I drove back to the Spectrum, wishing I'd eaten there and gotten to bed early instead of spending my evening autographing leaves.

The radio in the sled played a Dixieland number I hadn't heard in ages. That, and the rain that came a moment later, made me feel lonely and more than a little sad. Traffic was light. I hurried.

*   *   *

The following morning, I sent a courier-gram to Marling of Megapei, telling him to rest easy in the knowledge that Shimbo would be with him before the fifth season, and asking him if he knew a

Pei'an named Green Green, or some equivalent thereof, who might in any way be associated with the Name Belion. I asked him to reply by courier-gram, reverse-charge, and send his answer to Lawrence J. Conner, c/o Homefree, and I didn't sign it. I planned on leaving Driscoll for Homefree that same day. A courier-gram is about the fastest and one of the most expensive ways there is of sending an interstellar message; and even so, I knew there would be a lapse of a couple of weeks before I received a reply.

It was true that I was running a small risk of blowing my cover on Driscoll by sending a message of that class with a Homefree return on it, but I was leaving that day and I wanted to expedite things.

I checked out of the hotel and drove to the place on Nuage, to give it a final once-over, stopping for a late breakfast on the way.

I found only one thing new at the Raspberry Palace. There was something in the message-slot. It was a wide envelope, bearing no return address.

The envelope was for "Francis Sandow, c/o Ruth Laris." I took it inside with me and did not open it until I'd satisfied myself that there were no lurkers. Then I repocketed a tiny tube, capable of producing instant, silent and natural-seeming death, seated myself and opened my mail.

Yes.

Another picture.

It was Nick, my old friend Nick, Nick the dwarf, dead Nick, snarling through his beard and ready to leap at the photographer, standing there on a rocky ledge.

"Come visit Illyria. All your friends live there," said a note, in English.

I lit my first cigarette of the day.

Malisti, Bayner and DuBois knew who Lawrence John Conner was.

Malisti was my man on Driscoll, and I paid him enough so that he was, I thought, above bribery. Admitted, other pressures can be brought to bear on a man—but he himself had only learned my true identity the day before, when *Baa-baa blacksheep* had provided the key for the decoding of a special instruction. Not much time had passed in which to apply pressure.

Bayner had nothing, really, to gain by bugging me. We were partners in a joint venture which represented one of those drops in those buckets people talk about. That was all. Our fortunes were such that, even if our interests did conflict on occasion, it was a very impersonal thing. He was out.

DuBois didn't impress me as the sort to give away my name either, not after the way I'd spoken in his office concerning my willingness to resort to extreme means to obtain what I wanted.

Nobody at Homefree had known where I was going, except for S & F, whose memory of the fact I'd erased prior to my departure.

I considered an alternative.

If Ruth had been kidnapped, forced to write the note she had written, then whoever had taken her could safely assume I'd receive this latest if I responded, and if not, no harm done.

This seemed possible, probable.

So it meant there was somebody on Driscoll whose name I'd like to know.

Was it worth sticking around for? With Malisti on the job, I might be able to ferret out the sender of the latest picture.

But if there was a man behind the man and he was smart, his subordinate would know very little, might even be a totally innocent party. I resolved to put Malisti on the trail and have him send his findings to Homefree. I'd use a phone other than the one at my right hand, however.

In just a few hours, it wouldn't matter who knew that Conner was Sandow. I'd be on my way, and I'd never be Conner again.

*   *   *

"Everything that's miserable in the world," Nick the dwarf once said to me, "is because of beauty."

"Not truth or goodness?" I'd asked.

"Oh, they help. But beauty is the culprit, the real principle of evil."

"Not wealth?"

"Money is beautiful."

"So is anything else you don't have enough of—food, water, screwing . . ."

"Exactly!" he announced, slamming his beer mug down so heavily on the tabletop that a dozen heads were turned in our direction. "Beauty, goddamn it!"

"What about a good-looking guy?"

"They're either bastards because they know they've got it made, or they're self-conscious because they know other guys hate their guts. Bastards are always hurting other people, and the self-conscious guys screw themselves up. Usually they go queer or something, all because of that goddamn beauty!"

"What about beautiful objects?"

"They make people steal, or feel bad because they can't get at them. Damn—!"

"Wait a minute," I said. "It's not an object's fault that it's beautiful, or the pretty people's fault that they're pretty. It just happens that way."

He shrugged.

"Fault? Who said anything about fault?"

"You were talking about evil. That implies guilt somewhere along the line."

"Then beauty is guilty," he said. "Goddamn it!"

"Beauty, as an abstract principle?"

"Yes."

"And in individual objects?"

"Yes."

"That's ridiculous! Guilt requires responsibility, some kind of intent—"

"Beauty's responsible!"

"Have another beer."

He did, and belched again.

"Take a look at that good-looking guy over at the bar," he said, "that guy trying to pick up the broad in the green dress. Somebody's going to bust him one in the nose sometime. It wouldn't have to happen if he was ugly."

Nick later proved his point by busting the guy one in the nose, because he'd called him Shorty. So maybe there was something to what he said. Nick was around four feet tall. He had the shoulders and arms of a powerful athlete. He could beat anybody I knew at wrist-wrestling. He had a normal-sized head, too, full of blond hair and beard, with a couple blue eyes above a busted nose that turned off to the right and a mean smile that usually revealed only half a dozen of his yellow-stained teeth. He was all gnarled below the waist. He'd come from a family lousy with professional soldiers. His father'd been a general, and all of his brothers and sisters except for one were officers in something or other. Nick had grown up in an environment alive with the martial arts. Any weapon you cared to name, he could operate it. He could fence, shoot, ride, set explosive charges, break boards and necks with his hands, live off the land, and fail any physical examination in the galaxy because he was a dwarf. I'd hired him as a game hunter, to kill off my experiments that went bad. He hated beautiful things and things that were bigger than he was.

"What I think is beautiful and what you think is beautiful," I said, "might disgust a Rigelian, and vice-versa. Therefore, beauty is a relative thing. So you can't condemn it as an abstract principle if—"

"Crap!" he said. "So they hurt, rape, steal and screw themselves up over different things. It's still because beauty sits there demanding violation."

"Then how can you blame an individual object—"

"We do business with Rigelians, don't we?"

"Yes."

"Then it can be translated. Enough said."

Then the good-looking guy at the bar who'd been trying to pick up the broad in the green dress passed by on his way to the Men's Room and called Nick Shorty when he asked him to move his chair out of the way. That ended our evening in that bar.

Nick swore he'd die with his boots on, on some exotic safari, but he found his Kilimanjaro in a hospital on Earth, where they'd cured everything that was bothering him, except for the galloping pneumonia he'd picked up in the hospital.

That had been, roughly, two hundred and fifty years ago. I'd been a pallbearer.

*   *   *

I mashed out my cigarette and made my way back to the slip-sled. Whatever was rotten in Midi, I'd find it out later. It was time to go.

The dead are too much with us.

*   *   *

For two weeks, I puzzled over what I'd found and I kept myself fit. When I entered the Homefree system, my life was further complicated by the fact that Homefree had picked up an additional satellite. Not a natural one, either.

WHAT THE HELL, EXCLAMATION, I sent ahead in code.

VISITOR, came the reply. LANDING PERMISSION REQUESTED STOP DENIED STOP STILL CIRCLING STOP SAYS HES AN EARTH INTELLIGENCE MAN STOP

LET HIM LAND, I said, HALF A HOUR AFTER IM DOWN STOP

There came the acknowledgment, and I swung into a tight orbit and pushed the *Model T* down and around and down.

After a frolic with the beasts, I repaired to my home for a shower, shucked my Conner face, then dressed for dinner.

It would appear that something finally meant enough to the wealthiest government in existence for someone to at last authorize a trip on the part of some underpaid civil servant in one of the cheapest interstellar vehicles available.

I vowed to at least feed him well.

III

LEWIS BRIGGS and I regarded one another across the remains of dinner and the wide table they occupied. His identification papers informed me that he was an agent of Earth's Central Intelligence Department. He looked like a shaved monkey. He was a wizened little guy with a perpetually inquisitive stare, and it seemed as if he must be pushing retirement age. He'd stuttered just a bit when he'd introduced himself, but the dinner appeared to have relaxed him and the falter had halted.

"It was a very pleasant meal, Mister Sandow," he acknowledged. "Now, if I may, I'd like to discuss the business that brought me here."

"Then let's adjourn to the upstairs, where we can get some fresh air while we talk."

We arose, taking our drinks with us, and I led him to the elevator.

Five seconds later, it admitted us to the roof

garden, and I gestured toward a couple lounging chairs set beneath a chestnut tree. "How about there?" I asked. He nodded and seated himself. A cool breeze came out of the twilight and we breathed it in and gave it back.

"It's quite impressive," he said, looking around the garden shadows, "the way you satisfy your every whim."

"This particular whim in which we're relaxing," I said, "is landscaped to make this place virtually undetectable by means of aerial reconnaissance."

"Oh, the thought hadn't occurred to me."

I offered him a cigar, which he declined. So I lit it for myself and asked him, "So what is it you want of me?"

"Will you consent to accompany me back to Earth and talk to my chief?" he asked.

"No," I said. "I've answered that question a dozen times, in as many letters. Earth grates on my nerves, it gives me a big pain these days. That's why I live out here. Earth is overcrowded, bureaucratic, unhealthy, and suffering from too many mass-psychoses to bother classifying. Whatever your chief wants to say, you can say for him; and I'll answer you, and you can take it back to him."

"Normally," he said, "these matters are handled at the Division level."

"Sorry about that," I replied, "but I'll foot the bill for a coded courier-gram from here, if it comes to that."

"The reply would cost the Department too much," he said. "Our budget, you know."

"For Chrissake, I'll pay it both ways then! Anything to stop cluttering my incoming basket with what is still strangely referred to as surface-carrier mail."

"God! No!" A tone of panic clung to his words. "It's never been done before, and the man-hours involved in determining how to bill you would be prohibitive!"

Inwardly, I wept for thee, Mother Earth, and the prodigies that had been wrought upon thee. A government is born, it flourishes, strong is its nationalism and great its frontiers, then comes a time of solidification, division of labor unto specialization, and the layers of management and chains of command, yes, and Max Weber spoke of this. He saw bureaucracy in the necessary evolution of all institutions, and he saw that it was good. He saw that it was necessary and good. While it may be necessary, put a comma after that word and after the last one add "God" and an exclamation point. For there comes a time in the history of all bureaucracies when they must inevitably parody their own functions. Look what the breakup of the big Austro-Hungarian machine did to poor Kafka, or the Russian one to Gogol. It drove them out of their cotton-picking minds, poor bastards, and now I was looking at a man who had survived an infinitely more inscrutable one until the end of his days was in sight. This indicated to me that he was slightly below average intelligence, emotionally handicapped, insecure, or morally suspect; or else he was an iron-willed masochist. For these neuter machines, combining as they do the worst of both father-image and mother-image—*i.e.*, the security of the womb and the authority of an omniscient leader—always manage to attract the nebbish. And this is why, Mother Earth, I wept inwardly for thee at that moment of the immense parade called Time: the clowns were passing, and everybody knows that inside, somewhere, their hearts are broken.

"Then tell me what you would like of me and I'll answer you now," I said.

He reached into his inside pocket and withdrew a sealed envelope bearing various security stamps, which I didn't bother examining too closely, even when he handed it to me.

"Should you not consent to accompany me back to Earth, I was instructed to deliver this to you."

"If I had agreed to go along, what would you have done with it?"

"Returned it to my chief," he said.

"So that he could hand it to me?"

"Probably," he said.

I tore it open and withdrew a single sheet of paper.

I held it close and squinted through the dim light. It was a list of six names. I kept my face under control as I read them.

They were all names of people I had loved or hated, and they were each of them, somewhere, the subject of a moldering obituary.

Also, they had all figured prominently in some recent photography I had been called upon to witness.

I puffed smoke, refolded the list, replaced it in the envelope and dropped it on the table between us.

"What does it signify?" I asked, after a time.

"They are all potentially alive," he said. "I request that you destroy the list at your earliest convenience."

"Okay," I said, and, "Why are they potentially alive?"

"Because their Recall Tapes were stolen."

"How?"

"We don't know."

"Why?"

"We don't know that either."

"And you came to me . . . ?"

"Because you are the only link we could find. You knew all of them—well."

My first reaction was disbelief, but I concealed it and said nothing. Recall Tapes are the one thing in the universe which I had always considered inviolate, unreachable, for the thirty days of their existence—and then they were gone forever. I tried to get hold of one once and failed. Their guardians were incorruptible, their vaults impenetrable.

And this was part of another reason why I don't visit Earth much any more. I don't like the idea of wearing a Recall Plate, even temporarily. Persons born there have them implanted at birth and they are required by law to wear them for as long as they remain on Earth. Persons moving to Earth for purposes of residing there are required to have them installed. Even a visitor must bear one for the duration of his stay.

What they do is monitor the electromagnetic matrix of the nervous system. They record the shifting patterns of a man's being, and each is as unique as a fingerprint. Their one function is to transmit that final pattern, at the moment of death.

Death is the trigger, the shot is the psyche, the target's a machine. It's an enormous machine, and it records that transmission on a strip of tape you can hold in the palm of your hand—all that a man ever was or hoped to be—weighing less than an ounce. After thirty days, the tape is destroyed. That's it.

In a small and classified number of cases over the past several centuries, however, that wasn't it. The purpose for the whole strange and costly setup is this: there are some individuals who, dying suddenly, on the planet Earth, at crucial points in significant lives, depart this lachrymose valley with information vital to the economy/technology/national interest of Earth. The whole Recall System is there for the purpose of retrieving such data. Even the mighty machine is not sufficiently sophisticated to draw this information from the recorded matrix, however. That is why every wearer of the Plate has a frozen tissue culture, somewhere. This culture is associated with the tape and held for thirty days subsequent to death, and both are normally destroyed together. Should Recall be necessary, an entire new body is grown from the culture, in an AGT (that's an accelerated growth tank), and this body duplicates the original in all things, save that its brain is a tabula rasa. On this clean plate, then, is superimposed the recorded matrix, so that the recalled individual possesses every thought and memory which existed in the original up until the moment of death. He is then in a position to supply the information which the entire World Congress has deemed to be of sufficient value to warrant Recall. An iron-clad security setup guards the entire system, which is housed in a quarter-mile square fortress in Dallas.

"Do you think I stole the tapes?" I asked.

He crossed and uncrossed his legs, looked away.

"You'll admit there's a pattern, and that it seems somehow related to you?"

"Yes. But I didn't do it."

"You'll admit that you were investigated and charged at one time for attempting to bribe a government official in order to obtain the tape for your first wife, Katherine?"

"It is a matter of public record, so I can't deny it. But the charges were dismissed," I said.

"True—because you could afford a lot of bad publicity and good lawyers, and you hadn't succeeded in obtaining the tape, anyway. It was later stolen, though, and it was years before we discovered that it hadn't been destroyed on the scheduled date. There was no way of linking it to you, or of obtaining jurisdiction in the place you were then residing. There was no other way of reaching you, either."

I smiled at his accent on the word "reaching." I, too, have a security network.

"And what do you think I would have done with the tape, had I obtained it?"

"You're a wealthy man, Mister Sandow—one of the few who could afford to duplicate the machinery necessary for Recall. And your training—"

"I'll admit I once had that in mind. Unfortunately, I didn't obtain the tape, so the attempt was never made."

"Then how do you explain the others? The subsequent thefts which occurred over several centuries, always involving friends or enemies of yours."

"I don't have to explain," I said, "because I don't owe you an explanation for anything I do. But I will tell you this: I didn't do it. I don't have the tapes, never had them. I had no idea up until now that they were missing."

But, Good Lord! *They* were the six!

"Then accepting that as true, for the moment," he said, "can you supply us with any sort of lead as to who might have had sufficient interest in these people to go to such extremes?"

"I cannot," I said, seeing the Isle of the Dead in my mind's eye, and knowing that I would have to find out.

"I feel I should point out," said Briggs, "that this case will never be closed on our books until we have been satisfied as to the disposition of the tapes."

"I see," I said. "Would you mind telling me how many unclosed cases you're carrying on your books at the present time?"

"The number is unimportant," he said. "It's the principle involved. We never give up."

"It's just that I heard there were quite a few," I said, "and that some of them are getting pretty moldy."

"I take it you won't cooperate?"

"Not 'won't.' Can't. I don't have anything to give you."

"And you won't return to Earth with me?"

"To hear your chief repeat everything you've just said to me? No thanks. Tell him I'm sorry.

Tell him I'd help if I could, but I don't see any way I can."

"All right. I guess I'll be leaving then. Thanks for the dinner."

He rose.

"You might as well stay overnight," I said, "and get a decent night's sleep in a comfortable bed before you shove off."

He shook his head.

"Thanks, but I can't. I'm on per diem, and I have to account for all the time I spend on a job."

"How do they calculate per diem when you're in subspace?"

"It's complicated," he said.

*   *   *

So I waited for the mailman. He's a big fac-machine who picks up messages beamed to Homefree and turns them into letters and gives them to S & F, who sorts them and drops them into my basket. While I waited, I made my preparations for the visit to Illyria. I'd followed Briggs every step of the way. I'd seen him to his vessel and monitored its departure from my system. I supposed I might see him again one day, or his chief, if I found out what had really happened and made it back home. It was obvious that whoever wanted me on Illyria had not set the thing up for purposes of throwing a party on my behalf. That's why my preparations mainly involved the selection of weapons. As I picked and chose from among the smaller of the deadlies in my arsenal, I thought some thoughts of Recall.

Briggs had been right, of course. Only a wealthy man could afford to duplicate the expensive Recall equipment housed in Dallas. Some research would be involved, too, for a few of the techniques were still classified. I sought candidates from among my competitors. Douglas? No. He hated me, but he wouldn't go to such elaborate ends to nail me if he ever decided it was worthwhile. Krellson? He'd do it, if he could; but I kept him under such close surveillance that I was certain he hadn't had the opportunity for anything of this magnitude. The Lady Quoil of Rigel? Virtually senile by now. Her daughters ran her empire and wouldn't humor such an expensive request for revenge, I was sure. Who then?

I checked my records, and they didn't show recent transactions. So I sent a courier-gram to the Central Registration Unit for that stellar district. Before the answer came back, however, I received Marling's reply to my message from Driscoll.

"*Come to Megapei immediately,*" it said, and that was all. None of the formal flourishes characteristic of Pei'an writing style were present. Only that single, bald statement. It was the keynote of urgency. Either Marling was worse off than he'd suspected or my query had struck something big.

I arranged for CRU's message to be forwarded to me in Megapei, Megapei, Megapei, and then I was gone.

IV

MEGAPEI. If you're going to pick a place to die, you might as well pick a comfortable one. The Pei'ans did, and I consider them wise. It had been a pretty desolate place, I'm told, when they found it. But they refurbished it before they moved in and settled down to the business of dying.

Megapei's around seven thousand miles through the middle, with two big continents in the northern hemisphere and three small ones to the south. The larger of the northern ones looks like a tall teapot tilted to pour (the handle broken at the top), and the other resembles an ivy leaf from which some hungry caterpillar took a big, northwestern bite. These two are about eight hundred miles apart, and the bottom of the ivy leaf dips about five degrees into the tropic zone. The teapot is around the size of Europe. The three continents in the southern hemisphere look like continents; that is to say, irregular chunks of green and gray

71

surrounded by a cobalt sea, and they don't remind me of anything else. Then there's lots of little islands and a few fairly large ones scattered all about the globe. The icecaps are small and keep pretty much to themselves. The temperature is pleasant, as the ecliptic and the equator are fairly close. The continents all possess bright beaches and peaceful mountains, and any pleasant habitation you care to imagine somewhere in between. The Pei'ans had wanted it that way.

There are no large cities, and the city of Megapei on the continent of Megapei, there on Megapei, is therefore not a large city. (Megapei the continent is the chomped ivy leaf. Megapei the city lies on the sea in the middle of the chomp.) No two habitations within the city are nearer than a mile from one another.

I orbited twice, because I wanted to look down and admire that handiwork. I still couldn't spot a single feature which I'd have cared to change. They were my masters when it came to the old art, always would be.

Memories poured back, of the gone happy days before I'd become rich and famous and hated. The population of the entire world was less than a million. I could probably lose myself down there, as once I had, and dwell on Megapei for the rest of my days. I knew I wouldn't. Not yet, anyhow. But sometimes it's pleasant to daydream.

On my second pass, I entered the atmosphere, and after a time the winds sang about me, and the sky changed from indigo to violet to a deep, pure azure, with little wisps of cirrus hovering there between being and nothingness.

The stretch on which I landed was practically Marling's back yard. I secured the ship and walked toward his tower, carrying a small suitcase. It was about a mile's distance.

As I walked the familiar trail, shaded by broad-leafed trees, I whistled once, lightly, and a bird-call mimicked my note. I could smell the sea, though I could not yet view it. All was as it had been, years before, in the days when I had set myself the impossible task and gone forth to wrestle the gods, hoping only for forgetfulness, finding something far different.

Memories, like stained slides, suddenly became illuminated as I encountered, successively, an enormous, mossed-over boulder, a giant *parton* tree, a *crybbl* (an almost-lavender greyhound-like creature the size of a small horse, with long lashes and a crown of rosy quills), which quickly bounded away, a yellow sail—when the sea came into view—then Marling's pier, down in the cove, and finally the tower itself, entire, mauve, serene, severe and high, above the splashing, below the sun-rich skies, clean as a tooth and far, far older than I.

I ran the last hundred yards and banged upon the grillwork that covered the arched way into the small courtyard.

After perhaps two minutes, a strange young Pei'an came and stood and regarded me from the other side. I spoke to him in Pei'an. I said: "My name is Francis Sandow, and I have come to see *Dra* Marling." At this, the Pei'an unlatched the gate and held it open. Not until I had entered (for such is their custom) did he answer: "You are welcome, *Dra* Sandow. *Dra* Marling will see you after the tidal bell has rung. Let me show you to a place of rest and bring you refreshment." I thanked him and followed him up the winding stair.

I ate a light meal in the chamber to which he had conducted me. I still had more than an hour until the turning of the tide, so I lit a cigarette and stared out over the ocean through that wide, low window beside the bed, my elbows upon the sill that was harder than intermetallide plastic, and gray.

Strange to live like this, you say? A race capable of damn near anything, a man named Marling capable of building worlds? Maybe. Marling could have been wealthier than Bayner and I put together and multiplied by ten, had he chosen. But he'd picked a tower on a cliff overlooking the sea, a forest at his back, and he decided to live there till he died, and was doing it. I will trace no morals, such as a drawing away from the overcivilized races who were flooding the galaxy, such as repugnance for any society at all, even that of one's fellows. Anything would be an oversimplification. He was there because he wanted to be there, and I cannot go behind the fact. Still, we are kindred spirits, Marling and I, despite the differences in our fortresses. He saw that before I did, though how he could tell that the power might dwell in the broken alien who'd turned up on his doorstep one day, centuries before, is something that I do not understand.

Sick of wandering, frightened by Time, I had gone to seek counsel of what was said to be the oldest race around. How frightened I had become, I find it hard to describe. To see everything die—I don't think you know what it's like. But that's why I went to Megapei. Shall I tell you a little of myself? Why not? I told me again, as I waited for the bell.

I was born on the planet Earth, into the middle of the twentieth century, that period in the history of the race when man succeeded in casting off many of the inhibitions and taboos laid upon him by tradition, reveled for a brief time, and then discovered that it didn't make a bloody bit of difference that he had. He was still just as dead when he died, and he still was faced with every life-death problem that had confronted him before, compounded by the fact that Malthus was right. I left my indefinite college major at the end of my sophomore year to enlist in the Army, along with my younger brother who was just out of high school. That's how I found Tokyo Bay. Afterwards, I returned to school for a degree in engineering, decided that was a mistake, returned again to pick up the requirements for medical school. Somewhere along the line, I got sidetracked by the life sciences, went on for a master's in Biology, kept pursuing a growing interest in ecology. I was twenty-six years old and the year was 1991. My father had died and my mother had remarried. I had fallen for a girl, proposed to her, been rebuffed, volunteered for one of the first attempts to reach another star system. My mixed academic background got me passage, and I was frozen for a century's voyage. We made it to Burton, began setting up a colony. Before a year's time, however, I was stricken by a local disease for which we lacked a cure, not to mention a name. I was then refrozen in my cold bunker, to await some eventual therapy. Twenty-two years later, I came around. There had been eight more shiploads of colonists and a new world lay about me. Four more shiploads arrived that same year, and only two would remain. The other two were going on to a more distant system, to join an even newer colony. I got passage by trading places with a colonist who'd chickened out on the second leg of the flight. It was a once-in-a-lifetime opportunity, or so I thought, and since I could no longer recall the face—let alone the name—of the girl who had caused me to make the initial move, my desire to go on was predicated, I am certain, solely upon curiosity and the fact that the environment in which I then found myself had already been somewhat tamed, and I had had no part in its taming. It took a century and a quarter of cold sleep to reach the world we then sought, and I didn't like the place at all. That's why I signed up for a long haul, after only eight months—a two hundred seventy-six year journey out to Bifrost, which was to be man's farthest outpost, if we could make a go of it. Bifrost was bleak and bitter and scared me, and convinced me that maybe I wasn't meant to be a colonist. I made one more trip to get away, and it was already too late. People were suddenly all over the place, intelligent aliens were contacted, interstellar trips were matters of weeks and months, not centuries. Funny? I thought so. I thought it was a great joke. Then it was pointed out to me that I was possibly the oldest man alive, doubtless the only survivor of the twentieth century. They told me about the Earth. They showed me pictures. Then I didn't laugh any more, because Earth had become a different world. I was suddenly very alone. Everything I had learned in school seemed medieval. So what did I do? I went back to see for myself. I returned to school, discovered I could still learn. I was scared, though, all the time. I felt out of place. Then I heard of the one thing that might give me a wedge in the times, the one thing that might save me the feeling of being the last survivor of Atlantis walking down Broadway, the one thing that might make me superior to the strange world in which I found myself. I heard of the Pei'ans, a then recently discovered race to whom all the marvels of the twenty-seventh century on Earth—including the treatments which had added a couple centuries to my life-expectancy —would seem like ancient history. So I came to Megapei, Megapei, Megapei, half out of my mind, picked a tower at random, called out at the gate till someone responded, then said, "Teach me, please."   .

I had gone to the tower of Marling, all unknowing at the time—Marling, of the twenty-six Names that lived.

When the tidal bell rang, the young Pei'an came for me and he conducted me up the winding stair to the top. He stepped into the room, and I heard Marling's voice greet him.

"*Dra* Sandow is here to see you," he replied.

"Then bid him enter."

The young Pei'an returned through the door and said, "He bids you enter."

"Thank you."

I went in.

Marling was seated with his back to me, facing out the window toward the sea, as I knew he would be. The three large walls of his fan-shaped chamber were a pale green, resembling jade, and his bed was long, low and narrow. One wall was an enormous console, somewhat dusty. And the small, bedside table, which might not have been moved in centuries, still held the orange figurine resembling a horned dolphin leaping.

"*Dra*, good afternoon," I said.

"Come over here where I can see you."

I rounded his chair and stood before him. He was thinner and his skin was darker.

"You came quickly," he said, his eyes moving across my face.

I nodded.

"You said 'immediately.' "

He made a hissed, rattling sound, which is a Pei'an chuckle, then, "How have you been treating life?"

"With respect, deference and fear."

"What of your work?"

"I'm between jobs just now."

"Sit down."

He indicated a bench alongside the window, and I crossed to it.

"Tell me what has happened."

"Pictures," I said. "I've been receiving pictures of people I used to know—people who have been dead for some time now. All of them died on Earth, and I recently learned that their Recall Tapes were stolen. So it's possible that they *are* alive, somewhere. Then I received this."

I handed him the letter signed "Green Green."
He held it close and read it slowly.

"Do you know where the Isle of the Dead is?"
he asked.

"Yes; it's on a world I made."

"You are going?"

"Yes. I must."

"Green Green is, I believe, Gringrin-tharl of
the city Dilpei. He hates you."

"Why? I don't even know him."

"That is unimportant. Your existence offends
him, so naturally he wishes to be avenged for this
affront. It is sad."

"I'd say so. Especially if he succeeds. But how
has my existence served to offend him?"

"You are the only alien to be a Name-bearer. At
one time it was thought that none but a Pei'an
could master the art you have learned—and not
too many Pei'ans are capable, of course. Gringrin
undertook the study and he completed it. He was
to have been the twenty-seventh. He failed the
final test, however."

"The *final* test? I'd thought that one pretty much
a matter of form."

"No. It may have seemed so to you, but it is
not. So, after half a century of study with Delgren
of Dilpei, he was not confirmed in the trade. He
was somewhat exercised. He spoke often of the
fact that the last man to be admitted was not even
Pei'an. Then he departed Megapei. With his training, of course, he soon grew wealthy."

"How long ago was that?"

"Several hundred years. Perhaps six."

"And you feel he's been hating me all this time, and planning revenge?"

"Yes. There was no great hurry, and a good piece of revenge requires elaborate preparation."

It is always strange to hear a Pei'an speak so. Eminently civilized, they nevertheless have made revenge a way of life. It is doubtless another of the reasons why there are so few Pei'ans. Some of them actually keep vengeance books—long, elaborate lists of those who require a comeuppance—in order to keep track of everyone they intend to punish, complete with progress reports on the status of each vengeance scheme. A piece of vengeance isn't worth much to a Pei'an unless it's complicated, carefully planned and put into motion, and occurs with fiendish precision many years after the affront which stimulated it. It was explained to me that the fun of it is really in the planning and the anticipation. The actual death, madness, disfigurement or humiliation which results is quite secondary to this. Marling once confided in me that he had had three going which had lasted over a thousand years apiece, and that's no record. It's a way of life, really. It comforts one, providing a cheering object of contemplation when all other things are going poorly; it renders a certain satisfaction as the factors line themselves up, one by one—little triumphs, as it were—leading up to the time of fulfillment; and there is an esthetic pleasure to be had—some even say a mystical experience—when the situation occurs and the carefully wrought boom is lowered. Children are taught the system at an early age, for full familiarity with it is necessary for attaining advanced old age. I had had to learn it in a hurry, and was still weak on some of the finer points.

"Have you any suggestions?" I asked.

"Since it is useless to flee the vengeance of a Pei'an," he told me, "I would recommend your locating him immediately and challenging him to a walk through the night of the soul. I will provide you with some fresh *glitten* roots before you leave."

"Thank you. I'm not real up on that, you know."

"It is easy, and one of you will die, thus solving your problems. So if he accepts, you will have nothing to worry about. Should you die, you will be avenged by my estate."

"Thank you, *Dra*."

"It is nothing."

"What of Belion, with respect to Gringrin?"

"He is there."

"How so?"

"They have made their own terms, those two."

"And . . . ?"

"That is all I know."

"Will he see fit to walk with me, do you think?"

"I do not know."

Then, "Let us regard the waters in their rising," he said, and I turned and did so until he spoke again, perhaps half an hour later.

"This is all," he said.

"There is no more?"

"No."

The sky darkened until there were no sails. I could hear the sea, smell it, and there was its black, rolling, star-flecked bulk in the distance. I knew that soon an unseen bird would shriek, and one did. For a long while, I stood in a pertinent corner of my mind, examining things I had left there a long time ago and forgotten, and some things which I had never fully understood. My Big Tree toppled, the Valley of Shadows faded and the Isle of the Dead was only a hunk of rock dropped into the middle of the Bay and sinking without a ripple. I was alone, I was absolutely alone. I knew what the next words that I would hear would be; and then, sometime later, I heard them.

"Journey with me this night," he said.

"*Dra . . .*"

Nothing.

Then, "Must it be *this* night?" I said.

Nothing.

"Where then will dwell Lorimel of the Many Hands?"

"In the happy nothing, to come again, as always."

"What of your debts, your enemies?"

"All of them paid."

"You had spoken of next year, in the fifth season."

"That, now, is changed."

"I see."

"We will spend the night in converse, Earthson, that I may give you my final secrets before sunrise. Sit down," and I did, at his feet, as in days far away through the smoke of memory seen and younger, younger by far. He began to speak and I closed my eyes, listened.

He knew what he was doing, knew what he wanted. This didn't keep me from being frightened as well as saddened, however. He had chosen me to be his guide, the last living thing that he would see. It was the highest honor he could pay a man, and I was not worthy of it. I hadn't used what he had given me as well as I might have. I'd screwed up a lot of things I shouldn't have. I knew he knew it, too. But it didn't matter. I was the one. Which made him the only person in the whole galaxy able to remind me of my own father, dead these thousand-plus years. He had forgiven me my trespasses.

The fear and the sadness . . .

Why now? Why had he chosen this time?

Because there might not be any other.

In Marling's estimation, I was obviously off on a venture from which I would probably not be returning. This, therefore, would have to be our final encounter. "Everyman, I will go with thee and be thy guide, in thy most need to go by thy side." —A good line for Fear, though Knowledge spoke it. They've a lot in common, when you stop to consider it.

And so the fear.

We did not speak of the sadness either. It would not have been proper. We spoke for a time of the worlds we had made, of the places we had built and seen populated, of all the sciences that are involved in the feat of transforming rubble into a habitation and, ultimately, we spoke of the art. The ecology game is more complicated than any chess game, goes beyond the best formulations of any computer. This is because, finally, the problems are esthetic rather than scientific ones. All the thinking power within the seven-doored chamber of the skull is required, true; yet a dash of something still best described as inspiration is really the determining factor. We dwelled upon these inspirations, many of which now existed, and the night sea-wind rose up so shrill and cold that I had to secure the windows against it and kindle a small fire, which blazed then like a holy thing in that oxygen-rich place. I can remember none of the words that were spoken that night. Only there, preserved within me, are the soundless pictures we shared, memory now, glazed over with distance and time. "This is all," as he'd said, and after awhile there was dawn.

He fetched me the *glitten* roots when the faint false-dawn occurred, sat for a time and then we made the final preparations.

About three hours later, I summoned the servants and ordered them to hire mourners and to send a party ahead into the mountains to open the family burial crypt. Using Marling's equipment, I sent formal messages to the other twenty-five Names Which Lived, and to those he'd specified among friends, acquaintances and relatives that he wished to be present. Then I prepared the ancient and dark green body he had worn, found my way down to the kitchen for breakfast, lit a cigar and walked by the bright seaside where purple and yellow sails once more cut the horizon, found me a small tidal pool, sat down beside it, smoked.

I was numb. That's the easiest way to put it. I had been there before—the place from which I had just returned—and, as before, I came away with a certain indecipherable scribbling upon my soul. I wished now for the sadness or the fear again— anything. But I felt nothing, not even anger. This would come later, though, I knew; but for the moment, I was too young or too old.

Why did the day bloom so bright and the sea

sparkle so before me? Why did the air burn salt and pleasant within me, and the life-cries of the wood come like music into my ears? Nature is not so sympathetic as the poets would have you believe. Only other people sometimes care when you close your doors and do not open them again. I would stay in Megapei Megapei Megapei and listen to the litany of Lorimel of the Many Hands while the thousand-year-old flutes covered it like a sheet a statue. Then Shimbo would walk into the mountains once again, in procession with the others, and I, Francis Sandow, would see the opening of the cavern and gray, charcoal, black, the closing of the crypt. I would stay a few days more, to help order my master's affairs, and then depart upon my own journey. If it ended the same way—well, that's life.

So much for nightthoughts at mid-morning. I rose up and returned to the tower to wait.

In the days that followed, Shimbo walked again. I remember the thunder, as in a dream. There was thunder and flutes and the fiery hieroglyphs of lightnings above the mountains, beneath the clouds. This time Nature wept, for Shimbo dragged the bell-pull. I recall the green and gray procession, winding its way through the forest to the place where the timber broke and the dirt gave way to stone. As I walked, behind the creaking cart, the headgear of a Name-bearer upon me, the singed shawl of mourning about my shoulders, I bore in my hands the mask of Lorimel, a strip of dark cloth across the eyes. No more would his light burn in the shrines, unless another was given the Name. I understand that it did burn for a moment, though, at the time of his passing, in every shrine in the universe. Then the last door was closed, gray, charcoal, black. A strange dream, is it not?

After it was all over, I sat in the tower for a week, as was expected of me. I fasted, and my thoughts were my own. During that week, a message came in from the Central Registration Unit, via Homefree. I didn't read it until Weeksend, and when I did, I learned that Illyria was now owned by the Green Development Company.

Before the day was over, I was able to ascertain locally that the Green Development Company was Gringrin-tharl, formerly of Dilpei, ex-student of Delgren of Dilpei who bore the Name Clice, Out of Whose Mouth Proceedeth Rainbows. I called Delgren and made arrangements to see him the following afternoon. Then I broke my fast and I slept, for a long, long time. There were no dreams that I can recall.

*   *   *

Malisti had uncovered no one, nothing, on Driscoll. Delgren of Dilpei was of very little assistance, as he had not seen his former pupil for centuries. He hinted that he might be planning a surprise for Gringrin should he ever return to Megapei. I wondered if the feeling and the plans were mutual.

Whatever, these things no longer mattered. My time on Megapei had come to an end.

I boosted the *Model T* into the sky and kept going until space and time ended for a space and a time. I continued.

*   *   *

I anesthetized and cut open the middle finger of my left hand, implanted a laser crystal and some piezoelectric webbing, closed the incision and kept the hand in a healant unit for four hours. There was no scar. It would sting like hell and cost me some skin if I used it, but if I were to extend that finger, clench the others and turn my palm upward, the beam it emitted would cut through a two-foot slab of granite. I packed rations, medical supplies, food, *glitten* root in a light knapsack, which I cached near the port. I would not need a compass or maps, of course, but some firesticks, a sheet of flimsy, a hand torch and some night-specs seemed advisable. I laid out everything I could think of, including my plans.

I decided not to descend in the *Model T*, but to orbit and ride in on a non-metallic drift-sled. I'd give myself an Illyrian week on the surface. I would instruct the *T* to descend at the end of that time and hover above the strongest power-pull nexus—and then return once every day after that.

I slept, I ate. I waited, I hated.

Then one day there came a humming sound, rising to a whine. Then silence. The stars fell like fiery sleet, then froze all about me. Ahead, there hung one bright one.

I ascertained Illyria's position and moved toward a rendezvous.

A couple lifetimes or days later, I regarded it: a little green opal of a world, with flashing seas and countless bays, inlets, lakes, fjords; lush vegeta-

tion on the three tropical continents, cool wood-
lands and numerous lakes on the four temperate
ones; no really high mountains, but lots of hills;
nine small deserts, for variety's sake; one hump-
backed river, half again the length of the Mis-
sissippi; a system of oceanic currents I was really
proud of; and a five hundred mile land bridge/
mountain range I had raised between two continents, just because geologists hate them as much
as anthropologists love them. I watched a storm-
system develop near the equator, move north-
ward, disperse its wet burden over the ocean. One
by one, as I drew nearer, the three moons—
Flopsus, Mopsus and Kattontallus—partly eclipsed
the world.

I set the *Model T* into an enormous, elliptical
orbit, beyond the farthest moon; and, hopefully,
also beyond the range of any detection devices.
Then I set to work figuring the problem of the
descents—my initial one, and those later ones, by
the vessel itself.

Then I checked my current position, set an
alarm and took a nap.

When I awoke, I visited the latrine, checked
the drift-sled, went over my gear. I took an ultra-
sonic shower and dressed myself in black shirt and
trousers, of a water-repellent synthetic the name
of which I can never remember, even though I
own the company. I put on what I call combat
boots, but what everyone else calls hiking boots
these days, and bloused the trousers up inside.
Then I clasped on a soft leather belt with a dark,
two-piece buckle which could become the handles
for the strangling-wire that tore loose through the

center seam. I hung a pistol-belt over that, to hold
a laser handgun at my right hip, and I hooked a
row of small grenades along the back. I wore a
pendant around my neck, with a spit-bomb inside,
and on my right wrist I strapped a chrono set for
Illyria and gimmicked to spray para-gas from nine
o'clock when the stem was pulled. A handkerchief,
a comb and the remains of a thousand-year-old
rabbit's foot went into my pockets. I was ready.

I had to wait, though. I wanted to descend at
night, drifting down like thistledown but black,
onto the continent Splendida, going to ground no
closer than a hundred, no further than three hundred miles from my destination.

I wriggled into the knapsack, smoked a cigarette
and worked my way back to the sled-chamber. I
sealed it off and boarded the sled. I pulled shut
the half-bubble, locked it about me, felt a tiny jet
of air just above my head, a small wave of warmth
just about my feet. I pushed the button that raised
the hatch.

The wall opened, and I stared down at the
crescent moon my world had become. The T would
launch me at the proper moment; the sled would
brake itself at the right time. I had only to control
the drift, once I'd entered the atmosphere. The
sled and I together would weigh only a few pounds,
because of the anti-grav elements in the hull. It
had rudders, ailerons, stabilizers; also, sails and
chutes. It's less like a glider than one assumes on
first hearing of it. It's more like a sailboat for use
on a three-dimensional ocean. And I waited in it
and looked down at the wave of night washing day

from Illyria. Mopsus moved into view; Kattontallus moved out of it. My right ankle began to itch.

As I was scratching it, a blue light came on above my head. As I fastened my belts, it went out and the red one came on.

As I relaxed, the buzzer sounded and the red light went out and a mule kicked me in the backside and there were stars all about, dark Illyria before me, and no hatch to frame them.

Then drifting, not down, but ahead. Not falling, just moving, and even that undetectable when I closed my eyes. The world was a pit, a dark hole. Slowly, it grew. The warmth had filled the capsule, and the only sounds were my heart, my breath, the air jet.

When I turned my head, I could not see the *Model T.* Good.

It had been years since I'd used a drift-sled for purposes other than recreation. And each time I had, like now, my mind skipped back to a predawn sky and the rocking of the sea and the smell of sweat and the bitter after-taste of Dramamine in my throat and the first *thud* of artillery-fire as the landing vehicle neared the beach. Then, as now, I'd wiped my palms on my knees, reached into my left sidepocket and touched the dead bunnysfoot there. Funny. My brother had had one, too. He would have enjoyed the drift-sled. He'd liked airplanes and gliders and boats. He'd liked waterskiing and skindiving and acrobatics and aerobatics—that's why he'd gone Airborne, which is probably why he Got It, too. You can only expect so much from one lousy rabbit's foot.

The stars blazed like the love of God, cold and

distant, as soon as I dropped the blackspot on the bubble and blocked out the light of the sun. Mopsus caught the light, though, and cast it down into the pit. She held the middle orbit. Flopsus was nearest the planet, but was on the other side just then. The three made for generally tranquil seas, and once in a score or so of years they'd put on a magnificent tidal display when all of them were in conjunction. Isles of coral would appear in sudden deserts of purple and orange, as the waters rolled back, humped up, became a green mountain, moved round the world; and stones and bones and fishes and driftwood would lie like the footprints of Proteus, and the winds would follow, and the temperature-shifts, the inversions, the fields in the clouds, the cathedrals in the sky; and then the rains would come, and the wet mountains would break themselves upon the land, as the fairy cities shattered and the magic isles returned to the depths and Proteus, God knows where, would laugh like thunder, as with each bright flash Neptune's whitehot trident dipped, sizzled, dipped, sizzled. Afterwards, you'd rub your eyes.

Now Illyria was moonbeams over cheesecloth. Somewhere, in her sleep, a cat-like creature would stir soon. She would awaken, stretch, rise and begin to prowl. After a time, she would stare at the sky for a moment, at the moon, beyond the moon. Then a murmur would run through the valleys, and the leaves would move upon the trees. They would feel it. Born of my nervous system, fractioned from my own DNA, shaped in the initial cell by the unassisted power of my mind, they would feel it, all of them. Anticipation. —*Yes, my*

*children, I am coming. For Belion has dared to
walk among you. . . .*

Drifting.

If only it had been a man, there on Illyria,
waiting for me, it would have been easy. As it was,
I felt that my armaments were mainly trappings. If
it had only been a man, though, I wouldn't even
have bothered with them. But Green Green was
not a man; he was not even a Pei'an—which, in
itself, is a frightening thing to be. Rather, he was
something more than either.

He bore a Name, albeit improperly; and Name-
bearers can influence living things, even the elements about them, when they raise up and merge
with the shadow that lies behind the Name. I am
not getting theological. I've heard some scientific-
sounding explanations for everything involved, if
you'll buy voluntary schizophrenia along with a
god-complex and extrasensory faculties. Take them
one at a time, and bear in mind the number of
years' training a worldscaper undergoes, and the
number of candidates who complete it.

I had the edge on Green Green, I felt, because
it was my world he'd chosen for the encounter.
How long he'd had to fool around with it, of course,
was a thing I didn't know and a thing that worried
me. What changes had he effected? He'd chosen
the perfect bait. How perfect was the trap? How
much of an edge did he think he had? Whatever,
he couldn't be sure of anything, not against another Name. Nor, of course, could I.

Did you ever witness the combat of *betta
splendens,* the Siamese Fighting Fish? It's not like
a cock fight or a dog fight or a cobra-mongoose

match, or anything else in the world but itself. You place two males in the same bowl. They move together quickly, unfurling their brilliant fins, like red, blue, green shadows, expanding their branchial membranes. This gives the illusion of their suddenly blooming into something larger than they had been. Then they approach one another slowly, remain side by side for perhaps a quarter of a minute, drifting. Then they move, so fast that the eye can't even follow what is happening. Then, slow and peaceful again, they drift. Then suddenly, the colored whirlagig. Then drifting. Then movement. This pattern continues. The colored-shadow fins. And even this may be misleading. After a time, a reddish haze will surround them. Another flurry. They slow. Their jaws are locked. A minute passes, perhaps two. One opens his jaws and swims away. The other drifts.

This is how I saw what was to come.

I passed the moon, the dark bulk of the world grew before me, occluding stars. As I neared it, my descent slowed. Devices beneath the cockpit were activated, and when I finally entered the upper atmosphere I was already drifting, slowly. The impression of moonlight on a hundred lakes: coins at a dark pool's bottom.

I monitored for artificial light, detected none. Flopsus appeared upon the horizon, adding her light to her sister's. After perhaps half an hour, I could make out the more prominent features of the continent. I combined these with memory and feeling and began to steer the sled.

Like the falling of a leaf on a still day, tacking, sideslipping, I headed for the ground. The lake called Acheron, with its Isle of the Dead, lay, I calculated, some six hundred miles to the northwest.

Far below me, clouds appeared. I drifted on and they were gone. I lost very little altitude during the next half-hour and gained perhaps forty miles on my goal. I wondered what detection devices might be functioning below me.

The high-altitude winds caught me, and I fought them for a time; finally, though, I had to descend several thousand feet to escape the worst of them.

For the next several hours I made my way, steadily, north and west. At a height of some fifty thousand feet, I was still over four hundred miles from my goal. I wondered what detection devices might be functioning below me.

Within the next hour, though, I descended twenty thousand feet and gained about seventy miles. Things seemed to be breaking nicely.

Finally, a false dawn began in the east, and I dropped a mile to get beneath it. My speed increased as I did so. It was like descending into an ocean, light water to dark.

But the light followed me. After a time, I ran again. I plowed through a cloudbank, estimated my position, continued to descend. How many miles to Acheron?

Two hundred, perhaps.

The light caught me, passed me, went away.

I dropped to fifteen thousand feet, picked up forty miles. I deactivated several more plates.

I was cruising at three thousand feet when the real dawn began to occur.

I continued for ten minutes, dropping, found a clear place and went to ground.

The sun cracked open the east, and I was a hundred miles from Acheron, give or take around ten. I opened the bubble, pulled the destruct-cord, leapt to the ground and ran.

A minute later, the sled collapsed upon itself and began to smolder. I slowed to a walk, took my bearings, headed across the field toward the place where the trees began.

V

DURING THE first five minutes Illyria returned to
me, and it was as if I had never been gone. Filtered through the forest's mists, the sunlight came
rose and amber; dewdrops glistened on the leaves
and the grasses; the air was cool, smelled of damp
earth and decomposing vegetation, which is sweet.
A small yellow bird circled my head, lighted on
my shoulder, perched there for a dozen paces, was
gone. I stopped to cut myself a walking stick, and
the smell of the white wood took me back to Ohio
and the creek where I'd cut willows to fashion
whistles, soaking the wands overnight, tapping the
bark with the handle of my knife to loosen it, near
the place where the strawberries grew. And I
found some wild berries, huge and purple, crushed
them between my fingers and licked the juice,
which was tart. A crested lizard, bright as a to-
mato, stirred sluggishly atop his rock and moved
to sit on the toe of my boot as I was doing this. I

touched his crown, then pushed him away and moved on. When I looked back, his salt-and-pepper eyes met my own. I walked beneath forty- and fifty-foot trees, and moisture occasionally dripped down upon me. Birds began to awaken, and insects. A big-bellied green whistler began his ten-minute song of deflation on a limb above me. Somewhere to my left, a friend or relative joined in. Six purple *cobra de capella* flowers exploded from the ground and emitted hisses as they swayed upon their stalks, their petals rippling like flags, their heavy perfumes released with bomb-like efficiency. But I wasn't startled, for it was as if I had never gone away.

I walked on and the grasses diminished. The trees were larger now, ranging from fifty to seventy feet, with numerous boulders lying among them. A good place for an ambush; likewise, a good place to take cover from one.

The shadows were deep, and para-monkeys chanted overhead while a legion of clouds advanced from the west. The low sun tickled their quarters with flame, shot shafts of light through the leaves. Vines that clung to some of the giants held blossoms like silver candelabra, and the air about them hinted of temples and incense. I forded a pearly stream and crested water snakes swam beside me, hooting like owls. They were quite poisonous, but very friendly.

From the other bank, the ground began to slope upward, gently at first; and, as I advanced, some subtle change seemed to come over the world. There was nothing objective to which I could relate it, only a feeling that the decks of order had been slightly riffled.

The coolness of morning and the wood did not depart as the day advanced. Rather, it seemed to deepen. There was a definite chill in the air; and later it became an almost clammy feeling. Still, the sky was more than half-filled with clouds by then, and the ionization that precedes a storm often gives rise to such feelings.

When I stopped to eat, sitting with my back against the bole of an ancient mark-tree, I frightened a pandrilla who had been digging among its roots. As soon as he began to flee, I knew that something was wrong.

I filled my mind with the desire that he return, and laid it upon him.

He halted then in his flight and turned and regarded me. Slowly, he approached. I fed him a cracker and tried to see through his eyes as he ate it.

Fear, recognition, fear . . . There had been a moment of misplaced panic.

It didn't belong.

I released him and he remained, content to eat my crackers. His initial response had been too unusual to dismiss, however. I feared what it indicated.

I was entering enemy territory.

I finished eating and moved on. I descended into a foggy vale, and when I left it the mists were still with me. The sky was almost completely overcast. Small animals fled before me, and I made no effort to change their minds. I walked on, and my breath was white, moist wings now. I avoided two power-pulls. If I were to use one, it could betray my position to another sensitive.

What is a power-pull? Well, it's a part of the makeup of everything with an electromagnetic field. Every world has numerous, shifting points in its gravitational matrix. There, certain machines or specially talented people can plug in and act as switchboards, batteries, condensors. Power-pull is a handy term for such a nexus of energy, a term used by people who can employ it in such a fashion. I didn't want to use one until I was certain as to the nature of the enemy, however, for all Name-bearers normally possess this capability.

So I let the fog dampen my garments and take the sheen from my boottops, when I could have dried out. I walked with my staff in my left hand, my right one free to draw and fire.

Nothing attacked me, though, as I advanced. In fact, after a time no living thing crossed my path.

I hiked until evening, making perhaps twenty miles that day. The dampness was all-pervasive, but there was no rain. I located a small cave in the foothills I was then negotiating, cast my flimsy—a ten by ten sheet of tough plastic material, three molecules in thickness—for insulation against the dirt and some of the dampness, ate a dry meal and slept, my gun near my hand.

*   *   *

The morning was as bleak as the night and the day before, and the fog had thickened. I suspected an intent behind it, and I moved cautiously. It struck me as just a bit too melodramatic. If he thought he was going to shake me up with shadow, mist, chill and the alienation of a few of my creatures, he was wrong. Discomfort just irritates me, makes me angry and fixes my determination to get at its source and deal with it as quickly as possible.

I slopped my way through much of the second day, topped the hills and began my downward trek. It was along about evening that I picked up a companion.

A light appeared off to my left and moved parallel to my own course. It hovered anywhere from two to eight feet above the ground, and its color varied from pale yellow through orange to white. It could have been anywhere from twenty to a hundred feet away at any given time. Occasionally, it disappeared; always, it returned. A will-o-the-wisp, sent to lure me into some crevass or marshy bog? Probably. Still, I was curious, I admired its persistence—and it was nice to have company.

"Good evening," I said. "I'm coming to kill whoever sent you, you know.

"But then you might just be marsh gas," I added. "In which case, you may dismiss my last remark.

"Either way," I went on, "I'm not in the mood to be led astray just now. You can take a coffee break if you'd like."

Then I began whistling *It's a Long Way to Tipperary*. The thing continued to pace me. I stopped and sheltered beneath a tree, to light a cigarette. I stood there and smoked it. The light hovered about fifty feet away, as if waiting. I tried to touch it with my mind, but it was as if there was nothing there. I drew my gun and thought better of it, reholstered it. I finished my cigarette, crushed it out, moved ahead.

Again, the light moved with me.

About an hour later, I made camp in a small clearing. I wrapped myself in my flimsy, my back against a rock. I built a small fire and heated some soup I'd brought along. The light wouldn't carry far on a night like this.

The will-o-the-wisp hovered just outside the circle of firelight. "Care for a cup of coffee?" I asked it. There was no reply, which was a good thing. I had only one cup with me.

After I'd finished eating, I lit a cigar and let the fire go down to embers. I puffed my cigar and wished for stars. The night was soundless about me, and the chill was reaching for my backbone. It had already seized my toes and was gnawing on them. I wished I'd thought to bring a flask of brandy.

My fellow traveler stood vigil, unmoving, and I stared back at him. If it wasn't a natural phenomenon, it was there to spy on me. Dared I sleep? I dared.

When I awoke, my chrono showed me that an hour and a quarter had passed. Nothing had changed. Not forty minutes later, either, nor two hours and ten minutes after that, when I awoke again.

I slept out the rest of the night and found it waiting in the morning.

This day was like the previous one, cold and blank. I broke camp and moved on, reckoning that I was about a third of the way to my destination.

Suddenly, there was a new development. My

companion moved from my left and drifted slowly ahead. It turned right then and hovered, about sixty feet before me. By the time I reached that spot, it had moved on, anticipating my path.

That was a thing I didn't like. It was as though the guiding intelligence were mocking me, saying, "Look here, old boy, I know where you're headed and how you intend getting there. Why don't you let me make the way a bit easier?" It was a successful mock, too, for it made me feel like a complete fool. There were several things I could do about it, but I didn't feel like doing them yet.

So I followed. I followed till lunchtime, when it politely halted until I was quite finished; till dinnertime, when it did the same.

Shortly thereafter, however, the light again changed its behavior. It drifted off to the left and vanished. I stopped and stood still for a moment, for I'd grown used to it. Was I supposed to have become so conditioned to following it all day that fatigue and habit would combine to lead me after it now, off my intended path? Perhaps.

I wondered how far it would lead me if I gave it the opportunity.

I decided that twenty minutes of walking after it would be quite enough. I loosened my pistol in its holster and waited for it to come again.

It did. When it repeated its previous performances, I turned and followed. It hurried ahead, waited for me to catch up, hurried on.

After about five minutes, a light rain began to fall. Though the darkness deepened, I could see without using my hand torch. Soon I was soaked all the way through. I cursed and sloughed along, shivering.

Approximately half a mile further along, wetter, colder, darker the day, stronger still the feeling of alienation, I was left alone. The light went out. I waited, but it did not return.

Carefully, I made my way to the place where I had last seen it, circling in from the right, gun in hand, searching with my eyes and my mind.

I brushed against a dry tree-limb and heard it snap.

"Stop! For the love of God! Don't!"

I threw myself to the ground and rolled.

The cry had come from right beside me. I covered that area from a distance of twelve feet.

Cry? Had it been a truly physical sound, or something within my mind? I wasn't certain.

I waited.

Then, so softly that I wasn't certain how I was hearing it, there came to me a sound of sobbing. Soft sounds are difficult to pinpoint, and this was no exception. I turned my head slowly, from right to left, saw no one.

"Who is it?" I asked in a shrill whisper, for these, too, are without direction.

No answer. But the sobbing continued. Reaching out with my mind, I felt pain and confusion, nothing more.

"Who is it?" I repeated.

There was silence, then, "Frank?" said the voice.

This time I decided to wait. I let a minute go by, then said my name.

"Help me," came the reply.

"Who are you? Where are you?"

"Here. . . ."

And the answers came into my mind, and the nape of my neck crawled and my hand tightened on the pistol.

"Dango! The Capel Knife!"

I knew then what had happened, but I didn't have guts enough to turn on my torch and take a good look. I didn't need to, though.

My will-o-the-wisp chose that moment to return.

It drifted-past me, rose high, higher, brightness increasing in intensity to a level far beyond anything it had exhibited earlier. It hovered at a height of fifteen or twenty feet and blazed like a flare. Below it stood Dango. He had no choice but to stand.

He was rooted to the spot.

His lean, triangular face bore a long, black beard and flowing hair that twined away among his limbs, his leaves. His eyes were dark and sunken and wretched. The bark that was a part of him bore insect holes, bird-droppings and char-marks of numerous small fires about the base. I saw then that blood dripped from the limb I had broken as I'd passed him by.

I rose, slowly.

"Dango . . ." I said.

"They're gnawing at my feet!" he told me.

". . . I'm sorry." I lowered the gun, almost dropped it.

"Why didn't he let me stay dead?"

"Because once you were my friend, and then you were my enemy," I said. "You knew me, well."

"Because of you?" The tree swayed, as if reaching after me. He began to curse me, and I stood there and listened as the rain mingled with his blood and soaked into the ground. We had been partners in a joint venture one time, and he'd tried to cheat me. I'd brought charges, he was acquitted and tried to kill me afterwards. I put him in the hospital, back on Earth, and he'd died in an auto accident a week after his discharge. He would have killed me if he'd gotten the chance—with a knife, I know. But I never gave him the chance. You might sort of say I helped his bad luck along when it came to the accident. I knew he'd never rest until he'd nailed me or was dead, and I didn't feel like getting nailed.

The raking light made his features look ghastly. He had the complexion of a mushroom and the eyes of an evil cat. His teeth were broken and there was a festering sore on his left cheek. The back of his head was joined with the tree, his shoulders merged with it and there were two branches which might contain his arms. From the waist down he was tree.

"Who did it?" I asked.

"The big green bastard. Pei'an. . . ." he said. "Suddenly, I was here. I don't understand. There was an accident . . ."

"I'll get him," I said. "I'm going after him now. I'm going to kill him. Then I'll get you out—"

"No! Don't go!"

"It's the only way, Dango."

"You don't understand what it's like," he said. "I can't wait. . . . Please."

"It may only take a few days, Dango."

". . . And he may get you instead. Then it'll be

never. Christ! How it hurts! I'm sorry about that deal, Frank. Believe me. . . . Please!"

I looked down at the ground and up at the light. I raised the gun and lowered it.

"I can't kill you any more," I said.

He bit his lip and the blood ran down his chin and into his beard and the tears came out of his eyes. I looked away from his eyes.

I stumbled backwards and began mumbling in Pei'an. Only then did I realize I was near a power-pull. I could feel it suddenly. And I grew taller and taller, and Frank Sandow grew smaller and smaller, and when I shrugged the thunders rumbled. When I raised my left hand they roared. When I drew it down to my shoulder the flash that followed blinded me and the shock raised my hair upon my head.

. . . I was alone with the smells of ozone and smoke, there, before the charred and splintered thing that had been Dango the Knife. Even the will-o-the-wisp was gone now. The rain came down in torrents and laid the smells to rest.

I staggered back in the direction from which I had come, my boots making sucking sounds in the mud, my clothes trying to crawl under my skin.

Somehow, somewhere—I don't remember exactly —I slept.

* * *

Of all the things a man may do, sleep probably contributes most to keeping him sane. It puts brackets about each day. If you do something foolish or painful today, you get irritated if somebody mentions it, today. If it happened yesterday, though, you can nod or chuckle, as the case may be. You've crossed through nothingness or dream to another island in Time. How many memories can be summoned up in a single instant? Many, it would seem. Actually, though, they're only a small fraction of those which exist, somewhere. And the longer you've been around, the more of them you have. So, once I have slept, there are many things which come to aid me when I wish to anesthetize a particular occurrence. This may sound callous. It is not. I do not mean that I live without pain for things gone by, without guilt. I mean that over the centuries I have developed a mental reflex. When I have been swamped emotionally, I sleep. When I awaken, thoughts of other days come forth, fill my head. After a time, memory the vulture circles closer and closer, then descends upon the thing of pain. It dismembers it, gorges itself upon it, digests it with the past standing to witness. I suppose it is a thing called perspective. I have seen many persons die. In many fashions. I have never been unmoved. But sleep gives memory a chance to rev its engine and hand me back my head each day. For I have also seen people live, and I have looked upon the colors of joy, sorrow, love, hate, satiation, peace.

I found her in the mountains one morning, miles from anywhere, and her lips were blue and her fingers were frostbitten. She was wearing a tiger-striped pair of leotards and she was curled into a ball beside a scrubby little bush. I put my jacket around her and left my mineral bag and my tools on a rock, and I never did recover them. She was delirious, and it seemed I heard her say the name "Noel" several times while I was carrying her back to my vehicle. She had some bad bruises and a lot of minor cuts and abrasions. I took her to a clinic where they treated her and kept her overnight. The following morning I went to see her and learned that she'd refused to supply her identity. Also, she seemed unable to supply any money. So I paid her bill and asked her what she was going to do, and she didn't know that either. I offered to put her up at the cottage I was renting and she accepted. For the first week, it was like living in a haunted house. She never talked unless I asked her a question. She prepared meals for me and kept the place clean and spent the rest of the time in her room, with the door closed. The second week she heard me picking at an old mandolin—the first time I'd touched the thing in months—and she came out and sat across the living room from me and listened. So I kept playing, for hours longer than I'd intended, just to keep her there, because it was the only thing in over a week that had evoked any sort of response. When I laid it aside, she asked me if she could try it, and I nodded. She crossed the room, picked it up, bent over and began to play. She was far from a virtuoso, but then so was I. I listened and brought her a cup of coffee, said "Good night" and that was it. The next day, though, she was a different person. She'd combed the tangles out of her dark hair and trimmed it. Much of the puffiness was gone from beneath her pale eyes. She talked to me at breakfast, about everything from the weather, the news reports, my mineral collection, music, antiques to exotic fishes. Everything excepting herself. I took her places after that: restaurants, shows, the beach— everywhere but the mountains. About four months went by like this. Then one day I realized I was beginning to fall in love with her. Of course, I didn't mention it, though she must have seen it. Hell, I didn't really know anything about her, and I felt awkward. She might have a husband and six kids somewhere. She asked me to take her dancing. I did, and we danced on a terrace under the stars until they closed the place down, around four in the morning. The next day, when I rose at the crack of noon, I was alone. On the kitchen table there was a note that said: *Thank you. Please do not look for me. I have to go back now. I love you.* It was, of course, unsigned. And that's all I know about the girl without a name.

When I was around fifteen years old, I found a baby starling beneath a tree while I was mowing the lawn in our back yard. Both its legs were broken. At least, I surmised this, because they stuck out at funny angles from its body and it sat on its backside with its tail feathers bent way up. When I crossed its field of vision, it threw its head back and opened its beak. I bent down and saw that there were ants all over it, so I picked it up and brushed them off. Then I looked for a place to put it. I decided on a bushel basket lined with freshly cut grass. I set the thing on our picnic table on the patio under the maple trees. I tried an eyedropper to get some milk down its throat, but it just seemed to choke on it. I went back to mowing the lawn. Later that day, I looked in on it and there were five or six big black beetles down in the grass with it. Disgusted, I threw them out. The next morning, when I went out with milk and an eyedropper, there were more beetles. I cleaned house once again. Later that day, I saw a huge dark bird perched on the edge of the basket. She went down inside, and after a moment flew away. I kept watching, and she returned three times within the half hour. Then I went **out** and looked into the basket and saw more beetles. I realized that she'd been hunting them, bringing them to it, trying to feed it. It wasn't able to eat, however, so she just left them there in the basket. That night a cat found it. There were only a few feathers and some blood among the beetles when I went out with my eyedropper and some milk the next morning.

There is a place. It is a place where broken rocks ring a red sun. Several centuries ago, we discovered a race of arthropod-like creatures called *Whilles*, with whom we could not deal. They rejected friendly overtures on the parts of every known intelligent race. Also, they slew our emissaries and sent their remains back to us, missing a few pieces here and there. When first we contacted them, they possessed vehicles for travel within their own solar system. Shortly thereafter, they developed interstellar travel. Wherever they went, they killed and they stole and then beat it back home. Perhaps they didn't realize the size of the interstellar community at that time, or perhaps they didn't care. They guessed right if they thought it would take an awfully long time to reach an accord when it came to declaring war on them. There is actually very little precedent for interstellar war. The Pei'ans are about the only ones who remember any. So the attacks failed, what remained of our forces were withdrawn, and we began to bombard the planet. The *Whilles* were, however, further along technologically than we'd initially thought. They had a near-perfect defense system against missiles. So we withdrew and tried to contain them. They didn't stop their raids, though. Then the Names were contacted, and three worldscapers, Sang-ring of Greldei, Karth'ting of Mordei and I, were chosen by lot to use our abilities in reverse. Later, within the system of the *Whilles*, beyond the orbit of their home world, a belt of asteroids began to collapse upon itself, forming a planetoid. Rock by rock, it grew, and slowly it altered its course. We sat, with our machinery, beyond the orbit of the farthest planet, directing the new world's growth and its slow spiral inward. When the *Whilles* realized what was happening, they tried to destroy it. But it was too late. They never asked for mercy, and none of them tried to flee. They waited, and the day came. The orbits of the two worlds intersected, and now it is a place where broken rocks ring a red sun. I stayed drunk for a week after that.

Once I collapsed in a desert, while trying to walk from my damaged vehicle to a small outpost of civilization. I had been walking for four days, without water for two, and my throat felt like sandpaper and my feet were a million miles away. I passed out. How long I lay there, I do not know. Perhaps an entire day. Then, what I thought to be a product of delirium came and crouched beside me. It was purplish in color, with a ruff around its neck and three horny knobs on its lizard-like face. It was about four feet in length and scaly. It had a short tail and there were claws on each of its digits. Its eyes were dark ellipses with nictitating membranes. It carried a long, hollow reed and a small pouch. I still don't know what it was. It regarded me for a few moments, then dashed away. I rolled onto my side and watched it. It poked the reed into the ground and held its mouth over the end, then withdrew the reed, moved on and repeated the activity. About the eleventh time it did it, its cheeks began to bulge like balloons. Then it ran to my side, leaving the reed in place, and it touched my mouth with its forelimb. I guessed what it was trying to indicate and I opened my mouth. Leaning close, slowly, carefully, so as not to waste a drop, it trickled the hot, dirty water from its mouth into my own. Six times it returned to the reed and brought back water, giving it to me in this fashion. Then I passed out again. When I awakened, it was evening and the creature brought me more water. In the morning, I was able to walk to the tube, crouch beside it and draw my fill of liquid. The creature awakened slowly, sluggish in the pre-dawn cold. When it had come around, I took off my chrono and my hunting knife and I emptied my pockets of money and placed these things before it. It studied the items. I pushed them toward it and pointed at the pouch it bore. It pushed them back toward me and made a clicking sound with its tongue. So I touched its forelimb and said thanks in every language that I knew, picked up my stuff and started walking again. I made it into the settlement the following afternoon.

A girl, a bird, a world, a drink of water, and Dango the Knife riven from head to foot.

The cycles of recollection place pain beside thought, sight, sentiment and the always who-what-why? Sleep, the conductor of memory, keeps me sane. More than this I do not know, really. But I did not think I was callous by arising the following morning more intent upon what lay before me than behind.

* * *

What it was, was fifty to sixty miles of progressively difficult terrain. The ground was rockier, drier. Leaves possessed sharp, serrate edges.

The trees were different, the animals were different, from what I had left behind. They were parodies of the things in which I had taken such pride. My Midnight Warblers here emitted harsh croaking sounds, the insects all had stings and the flowers stank. There were no straight, tall trees. They were all of them twisted or squat. My gazelle-like leogahs were cripples. Smaller animals snarled at me and ran. Some of the larger ones had to be stared down.

My ears cracked with the increasing altitude and the fog was still with me, but I pushed on, steadily, and I made perhaps twenty-five miles that day.

Two more days, I figured. Perhaps less. And one to do the job.

That night I was awakened by one of the most god-awful explosions I'd heard in years. I sat up and listened to the echoes—or perhaps it was only the ringing in my ears. I sat there with my gun in my hand and waited, beneath a large, old tree.

In the northwest, despite the fog, I could see a light. It was a sort of generalized orange glow. It began to spread.

The second explosion was not so loud as the first. Neither was the third or the fourth. By then, however, I had other things to think about.

The ground was trembling beneath me.

I stayed where I was and waited. The shocks increased in intensity.

Judging from the sky, a quarter of the world was on fire.

Since there wasn't much I could do about it at the moment, I reholstered my pistol, sat with my back against the tree and lit a cigarette. Something seemed out of whack. Green Green was sure as hell going to a lot of trouble to impress me when he should have known I wasn't that impressionable. That kind of activity could not be natural in this region, and he was the only one other than myself who was on the scene and able to do it. Why? Was he just saying, "Look, I'm tearing up your world, Sandow. What are you going to do about it?" Was he demonstrating the power of Belion with hopes of frightening me?

I toyed for a moment with the notion of seeking out a power-pull and unleashing the worst electrical storm he'd ever seen, over the entire area, just to show him how impressed I was. But I shelved the idea quickly. I did not want to fight him from a distance. I wanted to meet him face to face and tell him what I thought of him. I wanted to confront him and show myself to him and ask him why he was being such a bloody fool—why my being a homo sap had aroused such a hatred that he'd gone to such lengths to hurt me.

He obviously knew I had already arrived, was there on the world somewhere—else there would have been no will-o-the-wisp to take me to Dango. So I betrayed nothing by what I did next.

I closed my eyes and bowed my head and summoned up the power. I tried to picture him somewhere near the Isle of the Dead, a gloating Pei'an, watching his volcano rise, watching the ashes spew forth like black leaves, watching the lava glow and boil, watching the snakes of sulfur crawl through the heavens—and with the full power of my hatred behind it, I sent forth the message:

"Patience, Green Green. Patience, Gringrin-tharl. Patience. In but a few days, I will be with you for a short time. A short time only."

There was no reply, but then I hadn't expected one.

In the morning, the going was rougher. A black snowfall of ashes descended through the mist. There was still an occasional tremblor, and animals fled past me, heading in the opposite direction. They ignored me completely, and I tried to ignore them.

The entire north seemed to be on fire. If it were not that I possess a sense of absolute direction on all my worlds, I would have thought that I was heading into a sunrise. I found it quite disillusioning.

Here was a Pei'an, almost a Name, a member of the most subtle race of avengers who had ever lived; and here he was acting like a clown before the abominable Earthman. Okay, he hated me and he wanted to get me. That was no reason to be sloppy about it and to forget the fine old traditions of his race. The volcano was a childish display of the power I fully expected to meet, eventually. I felt a bit ashamed for him, for such a crude exhibition at this point in the game. Even I, in my brief apprenticeship, had learned sufficient of the fine points of vengeanceship to know better than that. I was beginning to see why he'd flunked his test.

I chewed some chocolate as I walked, putting off lunch-break until later in the afternoon. I wanted to cover sufficient ground so that I'd only have a few hours' hike in the morning. I maintained a steady pace, and the light grew and grew before me, the ashes came more densely down, the ground gave a good shake about once every hour.

Around midday, a wart-bear attacked me. I tried to control it, but I couldn't. I killed it and cursed the man who had made it into what it was.

The fog had let up a good deal by then, but the drifting ash more than compensated. It was a constant twilight through which I walked, coughing. I didn't make good time because of the rearrangements of the terrain, and I added another day to my hiking schedule.

By the time I turned in that night I'd covered a lot of ground, though. I knew I'd reach Acheron before noon of the following day.

I found a dry spot for a campsite, on a small rise with half-buried boulders jutting at odd angles about its crown. I cleaned my equipment, pitched the flimsy, kindled a fire, ate some rations. Then I smoked one of my last cigars, to do my bit for air pollution, and crawled into the sack.

I was dreaming when it happened. The dream

eludes me now, save for the impression that it was pleasant at first, then became a nightmare. I remember tossing about on my bed of rushes, then realizing I was awake. I kept my eyes closed and shifted my weight as though moving in my sleep. My hand touched my pistol. I lay there and listened for the sounds of danger. I opened my mind to impressions.

I tasted the smoke and cold ashes that had filled the air. I felt the damp chill in the ground beneath me. I got the impression of someone, something, nearby. Listening, I heard the tiny click of a dislodged stone, somewhere off to my right. Then silence.

My finger traced the trigger's curve. I shifted the muzzle in that direction.

Then, as delicately as a hummingbird invades a flower, came the touch of the tamperer in the dark house where I live, my head.

You are asleep, something seemed to say, *and you will not awaken yet. Not until I permit it. You sleep and you hear me now. This is as it should be. There is no reason to awaken. Sleep deeply and soundly as I address you. It is very important that you do so . . .*

I let it continue, for I was fully awake. I suppressed my reactions and feigned slumber while I listened for another telltale sound.

After a minute of being reassured that I was asleep, I heard a sound of movement from the same direction as before.

I opened my eyes then, and without moving my head I began to trace the limits of the shadows.

Beside one of the rocks, perhaps thirty feet

distant, was a form which had not been present when I had retired. I studied it until I detected an occasional movement. When I was certain as to its position, I flipped off the safety catch, aimed very carefully and pulled the trigger, tracing a line of fire on the ground about five feet before it. Because of the angle, a shower of dust, dirt and gravel was kicked backwards.

If you so much as take a deep breath, I'll cut you in half, I advised.

Then I stood and faced him, holding the pistol steady. When I spoke, I spoke in Pei'an, for I had seen in the light of the burning beam that it was a Pei'an who stood beside the rock.

"Green Green," I said, "you are the clumsiest Pei'an I've ever met."

"I have made a few mistakes," he acknowledged, from back in the shadows.

I chuckled.

"I'd say so."

"There were extenuating circumstances involved."

"Excuses. You did not properly learn the lesson of the rock. It appears to rest, but it does move, imperceptibly." I shook my head. "How will your ancestors rest after a bungled piece of vengeance like this?"

"Poorly, I fear, if this be the end."

"Why shouldn't it be? Do you deny that you assured my presence here solely for purposes of obtaining my death?"

"Why should I deny the obvious?"

"Why should I fail to do the logical thing?"

"Think, Francis Sandow, *Dra* Sandow. How logical would it be? Why should I approach you in this fashion, when I might have allowed you to come to me where I held a position of power?"

"Perhaps I rattled your nerves last evening."

"Do not judge me that unstable. I came to place you under my control."

"And failed."

". . . And failed."

"Why did you come?"

"I require your services."

"To what end?"

"We must leave here quickly. You possess a means of departure?"

"Naturally. What are you afraid of?"

"Over the years, you have collected some friends and many enemies, Francis Sandow."

"Call me Frank. I feel as if I've known you a long time, dead man."

"You should not have sent that message, Frank. Now your presence here is known. Unless you help me to escape, you will face a vengeance greater than mine."

A shifting of the breeze brought me the sweet, musty smell of that which passes for blood in a Pei'an. I flicked on my hand torch and aimed it at him.

"You're hurt."

"Yes."

I dropped the torch, sidled over to my knapsack, opened it with my left hand. I fished out the first aid pouch and tossed it to him.

"Cover your cuts," I said, picking up the light once more. "They smell bad."

He unrolled a bandage and wrapped it about his

gashed right shoulder and forearm. He ignored a series of smaller wounds on his chest.

"You look as if you've been in a fight."

"I have."

"What shape is the other guy in?"

"I hurt him. I was lucky. I almost killed him, in fact. Now it is too late."

I saw that he wasn't carrying a weapon, so I holstered my own. I advanced and stood before him.

"Delgren of Dilpei sends his greetings," I said. "I think you've managed to make his fecal roster."

He snorted, chuckled.

"He was to be next," he said, "after yourself."

"You still haven't given me a good reason for keeping you alive."

"But I've aroused your curiosity, which is keeping me alive. Getting me bandaged, even."

"My patience departs, like sand through a sieve."

"Then you have not learned the lesson of the rock."

I lit a cigarette. "I'm in a position to choose my proverbs as I go along. You are not," I said.

He finished bandaging himself, then, "I wish to propose a bargain."

"Name it."

"You have a vessel hidden somewhere. Take me to it. Take me with you, away from this world."

"In return for what?"

"Your life."

"You're hardly in a position to threaten me."

"I am not making a threat. I am offering to save your life for the moment, if you will do the same for me."

"Save me from what?"

"You know that I can restore certain persons to life."

"Yeah, you stole some Recall Tapes.—How did you do it, by the way?"

"Teleportation. It is my talent. I can transfer small objects from one place to another. Many years ago, when I first began studying you and plotting my vengeance, I made visits to Earth— each time one of your friends or enemies died there, in fact. I waited then until I had accumulated sufficient funds to purchase this world, which I thought to be a fitting place for what I had in mind. It is not difficult for a worldscaper to learn to employ the tapes."

"My friends, my enemies—you restored them here?"

"That is correct."

"Why?"

"For you to see your loved ones suffer once again, before you died yourself; and for your enemies to watch you in your pain."

"Why did you do what you did to the one called Dango?"

"The man annoyed me. By setting him up as an example and warning for you, I also removed him from my presence and provided him with a maximum of pain. In this fashion, he served three useful purposes."

"What was the third?"

"My amusement, of course."

"I see. But why here? Why Illyria?"

"Second to Homefree, which is inaccessible, is this world not your favorite creation?"

"Yes."

"What better place then?"

I dropped my cigarette, ground it out with my heel.

"You are stronger than I thought, Frank," he said after a moment, "because you killed him once, and he has beaten me, taken away from me a thing without price. . . ."

Suddenly I was back on Homefree, in my roof garden, puffing a cigar, seated next to a shaved monkey named Lewis Briggs. I had just opened an envelope, and I was running my eyes down a list of names.

So it wasn't telepathy. It was just memory and apprehension.

"Mike Shandon," I said softly.

"Yes. I did not know him for what he was, or I would not have recalled him."

It should have hit me sooner. The fact that he had recalled all of them, I mean. It should have, but it didn't. I'd been too busy thinking about Kathy and blood.

"You stupid son of a bitch," I said. "You stupid son of a bitch. . . ."

*   *   *

Back in the century into which I had been born, like number twenty, the art or craft—as the case may be—of espionage enjoyed a better public image than either the U.S. Marine Corps or the AMA. It was, I suppose, partly a romantic escape mechanism with respect to international tensions. It got out of hand, though, as anything must if it is to leave a mark upon its times. In the long history of popular heroes, from Renaissance princes through poor boys who live clean, work hard and marry the bosses' daughters, the man with the cyanide capsule for a tooth, the lovely traitoress for a mistress and the impossible mission where sex and violence are shorthand for love and death, this man came into his own in the seventh decade of the twentieth century and is indeed remembered with a certain measure of nostalgia—like Christmas in Medieval England. He was, of course, abstracted from the real thing. And spies are an even duller lot today than they were then. They collect every bit of trivia they can lay their hands on and get it back to someone who feeds it to a data-processing machine, along with thousands of other items, a minor fact is thereby obtained, someone writes an obscure memo concerning it and the memo is filed and forgotten. As I mentioned earlier, there is very little precedent for interstellar warfare, and classical spying deals, basically, with military matters. When this extension of politics becomes well-nigh impossible because of logistics problems, the importance of such matters diminishes. The only real talented, important spies today are the industrial spies. The man who delivered into the hands of General Motors the microfilmed blueprints of Ford's latest brainchild or the gal with Dior's new line sketched inside her bra, *these* spies received very little notice in the twentieth century. Now, however, they are the only genuine items around. The tensions involved in interstellar commerce are enormous. Anything that will give you an edge—a new manufacturing process, a clas-

sified shipping schedule—may become as important as the Manhattan Project once was. If somebody
has something like this and you want it, a real spy
is worth his weight in meerschaum.

Mike Shandon was a real spy, the best one I'd
ever employed. I can never think of him without a
certain twitch of envy. He was everything I once
wished I could be.

He was around two inches taller than me and
perhaps twenty-five pounds heavier. His eyes were
the color of just-polished mahogany and his hair
was black as ink. He was damnably graceful, had a
sickeningly beautiful voice and was always dressed
to perfection. A farm boy from the breadbasket
world Wava, he'd had an itchy heel and expensive
tastes. He'd educated himself while being rehabil-
itated after some antisocial acts. In my youth, you
would have said he'd spent his free hours in the
prison library while doing time for grand larceny.
You don't say it that way any more, but it amounts
to the same thing. His rehabilitation was successful, if you judge it by the fact that it was a long
time before he got caught again. Of course, he had
a lot going for him. So much, in fact, that I was
surprised he'd *ever* been tripped up—though he
often said he was born to come in second. He was
a telepath, and he had a damn near photographic
memory. He was strong and tough and smart and
he could hold his liquor and women fell all over
him. So I think my certain twitch is not without
foundation.

He'd worked for me for several years before I'd
actually met him. One of my recruiters had turned
him up and sent him through Sandow Enterprises'

Special Executive Training Group (Spy School). A year later he emerged second in his class. Subsequent to that, he distinguished himself when it came to product research, as we call it. His name kept cropping up in classified reports, so one day I decided to have dinner with him.

Sincerity and good manners, that's all I remembered afterwards. He was a born con man.

There are not too many human telepaths around, and telepathically obtained information is not admissable in court. Nevertheless, the ability is obviously valuable.

Valuable as he might have been, however, Shandon was something of a problem. Whatever his earnings, he spent more.

It was not until years after his death that I learned of his blackmail activities. The thing that tripped him up, actually, was his moonlighting.

We knew there was a major security leak at SE. We didn't know how or where, and it took close to five years to find out. By then, Sandow Enterprises was beginning to totter.

We nailed him. It wasn't easy, and it involved four other telepaths. But we cornered him and brought him to trial. I testified at great length, and he was convicted, sentenced and shipped off for more rehabilitation. I undertook three world-scaping jobs then, to keep SE functioning smoothly. We weathered the vicissitudes that followed, but not without a lot of trouble.

. . .One item of which was Shandon's escape from rehabilitative custody. This was several years later, but word of it spread fast. His trial had been somewhat sensational.

So his name was added to the wanted lists. But the universe is a big place. . . .

It was near Coos Bay, Oregon, that I'd taken a seaside place for my stay on Earth. Two to three months had seemed in order, as I was there to watch over our merger with a couple North American companies.

Dwelling beside a body of water is tonic for the weary psyche. Sea smells, sea birds, seawrack, sands—alternately cool, warm, moist and dry—a taste of brine and the presence of the rocking, slopping bluegraygreen spit-flecked waters, has the effect of rinsing the emotions, bathing the outlook, bleaching the conscience. I walked beside it every morning before breakfast, and again in the evening before retiring. My name was Carlos Palermo, if anybody cared. After six weeks, the place had gotten me to feeling clean and healthy; and what with the mergers, my financial empire was finally coming back into balance.

The place where I stayed was set in a small cove. The house, a white, stucco building with red-tiled roof and an enclosed courtyard behind it, was right by the water. Set in the seaside wall was a black, metal gate, and beyond this lay the beach. To the south, a high escarpment of gray shale; a tangled mass of bushes and trees ended the beach to the north. It was peaceful, I was peaceful.

The night was cool—you could almost say chill. A big, three-quarter moon was working its way down into the west and dripping light onto the water. The stars seemed exceptionally bright. Far out over the heaving bulk of the ocean, a cluster of eight sea-mine derricks blocked starlight. A floating island occasionally reflected moonbeams from off its slick surfaces.

I didn't hear him coming. Apparently he had worked his way down through the brush to the north, waited till I was as near as I was going to be, approached as close as he could and rushed me when I became aware of his presence.

It is easier than you might think for one telepath to conceal himself from another, while remaining aware of the other's position and general activities. It is a matter of "blocking"—imagining a shield around yourself and remaining as emotionally inert as possible.

Admitted, this is rather difficult to do when you hate a man's guts and are stalking him for purposes of killing him. This, probably, is what saved my life.

I cannot really say that I realized there was a vicious presence at my back. It was just that as I took the night air and strolled along the line of the surf, I suddenly became apprehensive. Those nameless thoughts that sometimes run through the back of your head when you awaken for no apparent reason in the middle of a still, warm summer night, lie there awhile wondering what the hell woke you up, and then hear an unusual sound in the next room, magnified by the quiet, electrified by your inexplicable resurrection into a sense of emergency and stomach-squeezing tension—those thoughts raced in an instant, and my toes and fingertips (old anthropoid reflex) tingled, and the night seemed a shade darker and the sea a home for possible terrors whose sucking tentacles mingled with the wave even then heading toward me;

overhead, a line of brightness signified an upper-atmosphere transport which could any moment cease to function and descend like a meteor upon me.

So, when I heard the first, quick crunch of sand behind me, the adrenalin was already there.

I turned quickly, dropping into a crouch. My right foot skidded out behind me as I moved, and I fell to one knee.

A blow to the side of my face sent me sprawling to my right. He was upon me then, and we grappled in the sand, rolling, wrestling for position. Crying out would have been a waste of breath, for there was nobody else around. I tried to scuff sand into his eyes, I tried to knee him in the groin and jab him in any of a dozen painful places. He had been well trained, however, and he outweighed me and seemed faster, too.

Strange as it sounds, we fought for close to five minutes before I realized who he was. We were in the wet sand then, with the surf breaking about us, and he had already broken my nose with a forward smash of his head and snapped two of my fingers when I'd tried for a lock about his throat. The moonlight touched his moist face and I saw that it was Shandon and knew that I would have to kill him to stop him. A knockout would not be good enough. A prison or a hospital would only postpone another encounter. He had to die if I was to live. I imagine his reasoning was the same.

Moments later, something hard and sharp jabbed me in the back, and I wriggled to the left. If a man decides he wants to kill me, I don't much care how I do it to him. Being first is the only thing that matters.

As the surf splashed about my ears and Shandon pushed my head backwards into the water, I groped with my right hand and found the rock.

The first blow glanced off the forearm he had raised in defense. Telepaths have a certain advantage in a fight, because they often know what the other fellow is planning to do next. But it is a terrible thing to know and not be able to do a thing about it. My second blow smashed into his left eyesocket, and he must have seen his death coming because he howled then, like a dog, right before I pulped his temple. I hit him twice again for good measure, pushed him off and rolled away, the rock slipping from my fingers and splashing beside me.

I lay there for a long while, blinking back at the stars, while the surf washed me and the body of my enemy rocked gently, a few feet away.

When I recovered, I searched him, and among other things I found a pistol. It carried a full charge and was in perfect operating condition.

In other words, he'd wanted to kill me with his hands. He had estimated he was able to, and he had preferred risking injury in order to do it that way. He could have nailed me from the shadows, but he had had guts enough to follow the dictates of his hate. He could have been the most dangerous man I had ever faced, if he had used his brains. For this, I respected him. If it had been the other way around, *I* would have done it the easy way. If the reasons for any violence in which

I may indulge are emotional ones, I never let those feelings dictate the means.

I reported the attack, and Shandon lay dead on Earth. Somewhere in Dallas, he had become a strip of tape you could hold in the palm of your hand—all that he ever was or hoped to be—weighing less than an ounce. After thirty days, that too, would be gone.

Weeks later, on the eve of my departure, I stood on the same spot, there on the other side of the Big Pond from Tokyo Bay, and I knew that once you go down in it you do not come again. The reflected stars buckled and twisted, like in warp-drive, and though I did not know it at the time, somewhere a green man was laughing. He had gone fishing in the Bay.

*   *   *

"You stupid son of a bitch," I said.

VI

TO HAVE it all to do over again annoyed me. But
more than annoyance, there was a certain fear.
Shandon had slipped up, selling himself to his
emotions once. He would not be likely to make
the same mistake again. He was a tough, dangerous man, and now he apparently had a piece of
something which made him even more dangerous.
Also, he had to be aware of my presence on Illyria,
after my sending to Green Green earlier in the
evening.

"You have complicated my problem," I said, "so
you are going to help me resolve it."

"I do not understand," Green Green said.

"You baited a trap for me and it has grown more
teeth," I told him, "but the bait is just as much an
inducement now as it was before. I'm going after
it, and you're coming along."

He laughed.

"I am sorry, but my path leads in the opposite

direction. I will not go back willingly, and I would be of no use to you as a prisoner. In fact, I would represent a distinct impediment."

"I have three choices," I said. "I can kill you now, let you go your way, or allow you to accompany me. You may dismiss the first for the time being, as you are of no use to me dead. If you go your way, I will proceed as I began, on my own. If I obtain what I wish, I will return to Megapei. There, I will tell how you failed in your centuries-long plan of vengeance on an Earthman. I will tell how you dropped your plan and fled, because another man of that same race had scared the hell out of you. If you wish then to take wives, you must seek them from among your people on other worlds—and even there, the word may reach them eventually. None would call you *Dra*, despite your wealth. Megapei would refuse your bones when you die. You will never again hear the ringing of the tidal bells and know that they ring for you."

"May the blind things at the bottom of the great sea, whose bellies are circles of light," he said, "recall with pleasure the flavor of your marrow."

I blew a smoke ring. " . . . And if I should proceed as I began, on my own," I said, "and be slain myself in the coming encounter, do you think that you will escape from harm? Did you not look into the mind of Mike Shandon as you fought him? Did you not say that you hurt him? Do you not know that he is a man who will not forget such a thing? He is not so subtle as a Pei'an. He does not consider it necessary to proceed with finesse. He will simply turn and seek you, and when he finds you he will cut you down. So whether I win or lose, your end will be disgrace or death."

"If I elect to accompany you and assist you, what then?" he asked.

"I will forget the vengeance which you sought upon me," I said. "I will show you that there was no *pai'badra*, no instrument of affront, so that you may take leave of this vengeance with honor. I will not seek recompense, and we may go our ways thereafter, each freed of the hooks of the other."

"No," he said. "There was *pai'badra* in your elevation to a Name. I do not accept what you propose."

I shrugged. "Very well," I said, "then how does this sound? Since your feelings and intentions are known to me, it would be useless for either of us to plot vengeance along classical lines. That fine, final moment, where the enemy realizes the instrument, the mover and the *pai'badra* and knows then that his entire life has been but a preface to this irony— that moment would be diminished, if not destroyed.

"So let me offer you satisfaction rather than forgiveness," I went on. "Assist me, and I will give you a fair opportunity to destroy me afterwards. I, of course, will require an equal chance to destroy you. What do you say to that?"

"What means did you have in mind?"

"None, at the moment. Anything that is mutually agreeable will do."

"What assurance may I have of this?"

"I swear it by the Name that I bear."

He turned away and was silent for a time, then, "I agree to your terms," he said. "I will accompany you and assist you."

"Then let us move back to my campsite and become more comfortable," I said. "There are things you have hinted at which I must know more fully."

I turned my back upon him then and walked away. I knocked down the tent and spread the flimsy then for us to sit upon. I rekindled the campfire.

The ground shook very slightly before we seated ourselves upon it.

"Did you do that?" I asked him, gesturing toward the northwest.

"Partly," he replied.

"Why? Trying to frighten me?"

"Not you."

"And Shandon wasn't scared either?"

"Far from it."

"Supposing you tell me precisely what has happened."

"First, concerning our agreement," he said, "a counterproposal has just occurred to me—one in which you will be interested."

"What is it?"

"You are going there to rescue your friends." He gestured. "Supposing it were possible to recover them without peril? Supposing Mike Shandon could be avoided completely? Would you not prefer to do it that way?—Or do you require his blood immediately?"

I sat there and thought about it. If I let him live, he would come after me again sooner or later. On the other hand, if I could get what I wanted now without having to face him, I could find a thousand safe ways of taking him out of the game, afterwards. Still, I'd come to Illyria ready to face a deadly man. What difference did it make if the names and faces were changed? Still . . .

"Let's hear your proposal."

"The people you seek," he said, "are there only because I recalled them. You know how I did it. I used the tapes. These tapes are intact, and only I know where they are located. I told you how I obtained them. That which I did before I can do now. I can transport the tapes here immediately, if you so bid me. Then we can depart this place, and you can recall your people as you would. Once we are aloft in your vessel, I can show you where to burn or bomb to destroy Mike Shandon without danger to ourselves. Is this not simpler and safer? We can settle our own differences later, by agreement."

"There are two holes in it," I said. "One, there will be no tape for Ruth Laris. Two, I would be abandoning the others. Whether I can recall them again is unimportant, if I leave them behind me now."

"The analogues you recall will have no memory of this."

"That is not the point. They exist right now. They're as real as you or I. It does not matter that they can be duplicated. —They're on the Isle of the Dead, aren't they?"

"Yes."

"Then if I were to destroy it to get Shandon I'd get everybody, wouldn't I?"

"That would necessarily follow. But—"

"I veto your proposal."

"That is your privilege."

"Have you any other suggestions?"

"No."

"Good. Now that you've exhausted everything you have to change the subject, tell me what happened between you and Shandon back there."

"He bears a Name."

"What?"

"The shadow of Belion stands behind him."

"That's impossible. It doesn't work that way. He's no worldscaper—"

"Bide a moment, Frank, for I know it requires explanation. Apparently there are some things *Dra* Marling never saw fit to tell you. He was a revisionist, however, so it is understandable.

"You know," he continued, "that being a Name-bearer is not essential for the design and construction of worlds—"

"Of course it is. It is a necessary psychological device to release unconscious potentials which are required to perform certain phases of the work. One has to be able to feel like a god to act like one."

"Then why can I do the work?"

"I never heard of you before you became my enemy. I've never seen any of your work, save that which stands about me here, grafted onto my own. If it is representative, then I would say that you can't do the work. You're a lousy craftsman."

"As you would have it," he said. "Nevertheless, it is obvious that I can manipulate the necessary processes."

"Anybody can learn to do that. You were talking about creative design, of which I see no indication on your part."

"I was talking about the pantheon of Strantri. It existed before there were worldscapers, you know."

"I know. What of it?"

"Revisionists, like *Dra* Marling and his predecessors, used the old religion in their trade. They did not take it for its own sake, but, as you say, as a psychological device. Your confirmation as the Shrugger of Thunders was merely a means of coordinating your subconscious. To a fundamentalist, this is blasphemous."

"You are a fundamentalist?"

"Yes."

"Then why did you apprentice yourself to what you consider a sinful trade?"

"In order to be confirmed with a Name."

"I'm afraid you've lost me."

"It was the Name that I wanted, not the trade. My reasons were religious, not economic."

"But if it is only a psychological device—"

"That is the point! It is not. It is an authentic ceremony, and its results—personal contact with the god—are genuine. It is the ordination rite for the high priests of Strantri."

"Then why didn't you take holy orders, rather than world engineering?"

"Because only a Name may administer the rite, and the twenty-seven Names who live are all revisionists. They would not administer the rite for the old reasons."

"Twenty-six," I said.

"Twenty-six?"

"*Dra* Marling is under the mountain, and Lorimel of the Many Hands dwells in the happy nothing."

He lowered his head and was silent for a time. Then, "One less," he said. "I can remember when there were forty-three."

"It is sad."

"Yes."

"Why did you want a Name?"

"In order to be a priest, not a worldscaper. But the revisionists would not have one like me among them. They let me finish the training, then rejected me. Then, to insult me further, the next man they confirmed was an alien."

"I see. That is why you marked me for vengeance?"

"Yes."

"I was hardly responsible, you know. In fact, this is the first time I've heard the story. I had always thought that denominational differences meant very little within Strantri."

"Now you know better. You also must understand that I bear you no personal malice. By avenging myself on you, I strike back at those who blaspheme."

"Why do you indulge in what worldscaping you do, if you consider it immoral?"

"Worldscaping is not immoral. It is the subjugation of the true religion to this end that I find objectionable. I do not bear a Name in the orthodox sense of the term, and the work pays me well. So why should I not do it?"

"No reason I can think of," I told him, "if someone's willing to pay you to try. But what then is your connection with Belion, and Belion with Mike Shandon?"

"Sin and retribution, I suppose. I undertook the confirmation rite myself one night, in the temple at Prilbei. You know how it is, when the sacrifice is made and the words are spoken and you move along the outer wall of the temple, paying homage to each of the gods—how one tablet lights up before you and you feel the power come into you, and that is the Name you will bear?"

"Yes."

"It happened to me at the Station of Belion."

"So you confirmed yourself."

"He confirmed me, in his own Name. I did not want it to be him, for he is a destroyer, not a creator. I had hoped that Kirwar of the Four Faces, Father of Flowers, would come to me."

"Each must abide by his disposition."

"That is true, but I had gotten mine wrongly. Belion would move me even when I did not summon him. I do not know but that he may even have moved me in my vengeance-design for you, because you bear the Name of his ancient enemy. I can feel my thinking changing, even now as I speak of these things. Yes, it may be possible. Since he left me, things have been so different . . ."

"How could he leave you? The disposition is for life."

"But the nature of my confirmation may not have bound him to me. He is gone now."

"Shandon. . . ."

"Yes. He is one of the rare ones among your people who can communicate without words, such as yourself."

"I was not always so. The power grew in me slowly, as I studied with Marling."

"When I recalled him to life, the first thing that I saw in his mind was the anguish of his passing by your hand. But then, quickly, very quickly, he cast this off and became oriented. His mental processes intrigued me and I favored him above the others, some of whom had to be maintained as prisoners. I talked with him often and taught him many things. He came to assist me in the preparations for your visit."

"How long has he been around?"

"About a *splanth*," he said. (A *splanth* is around eight and a half Earth-months.) "I called them all back at approximately the same time."

"Why did you kidnap Ruth Laris?"

"I thought that perhaps you did not believe your dead had been recalled. There followed no massive search on your part after I began sending the pictures. It would have been enjoyable had you searched for a long while to find that this was the place. Since you did not respond, I decided to become more obvious. I kidnapped one of various people who meant something to you. Had you not responded after that, when I even took the trouble of leaving you a message, then I would have taken another, and another—until you saw fit to come looking."

"So Shandon became your protégé. You trusted him."

"Of course. He was a very willing pupil and assistant. He is intelligent and possesses a pleasing manner. It was pleasant having him about."

"Until recently."

"Yes. It is unfortunate that I misread his interest and cooperativeness. Quite naturally, he shared my desire for vengeance upon you. So, of course, did your other enemies, but they were not so clever and none of them telepaths. I enjoyed having someone here with whom I could communicate directly."

"What then caused the falling-out between two such fine friends?"

"When it happened yesterday, it seemed that it was the matter of the vengeance. Actually, though, it was the power. He was more devious than I had allowed for. He tricked me."

"In what fashion?"

"He said that he wanted more than your death as we had planned it. He said that he wanted *personal* vengeance, that he wanted to kill you himself. We argued over this. Finally, he refused to follow my orders and I threatened to discipline him."

He was silent for a moment, then continued: "He struck me then. He hit me with his hands. As I defended myself, the fury grew in me and I decided to hurt him badly before I destroyed him. I called upon the Name that I had taken and Belion heard and came to me. I reached a power-pull, and standing in the shadow of Belion I burst the ground at our feet and called up the vapors and flames that dwell at the heart of the world. This was how I almost slew him, for he tottered for a moment on the brink of the abyss. I scalded him badly then, but he recovered his balance. He had achieved his intention; he had forced me to summon Belion."

"What end did this serve?"

"He knew my story, even as I have told it to you. He knew how I had obtained the Name, and he had a plan concerning it which he had been able to conceal from me. Had I known of it, however, I would have been amused. Nothing more. When I saw what he was attempting, I laughed. I, too, believed that such things could not be. But I was mistaken. He made a pact with Belion.

"He had aroused me to anger and placed my life in jeopardy, knowing I would summon Belion if these things occurred and I was given sufficient time. He fought poorly, to give me that time. Then, when the shadow came over me and I stood as one apart, he reached out with his mind and there was communion. In this fashion did he gamble with his life for power. He said, had he spoken with words, 'Look upon me. Am I not a superior vessel to he whom You have chosen? Come number the ways of my mind and the powers of my body. When You have done this thing, You may choose to forsake the Pei'an and walk with me all the days of my life. I invite You. I am better suited than any man alive to serve Your ends, which I take to be fire and destruction. This one who stands before me is weak and would have consorted with the Father of Flowers had he been given a choice. Come over to me, and we both shall profit by the association.' "

Here he paused again.

"And?" I said.

"Suddenly I was alone."

Somewhere a bird croaked. The night manufactured moisture and began to paint the world with it. Soon a light would begin in the east, fade away, come again. I stared into the fire and saw no faces.

"Seems to shoot hell out of the autonomous complex theory," I said. "But I have heard of transferred psychoses among telepaths. It could be something like that."

"No. Belion and I were bound by confirmation. He found a better agent and he left me."

"I am not convinced that he is an entity in his own right."

"You—a Name-bearer—do not believe . . . ? You give me cause to dislike you."

"Don't go looking for new *pai'badra*, huh? Look where your last one got you. I only said that I'm not wholly convinced. I don't know. —What happened after Shandon made his pact with Belion?"

"He turned slowly from the fissure which had opened between us. He turned his back on me, as if I no longer existed. I reached out with my mind to touch him, and Belion was there. He raised his arms and the entire isle began to tremble. I turned and fled then. I took the boat from its mooring and headed for the shore. After a time, the waters boiled about me. Then the eruptions began. I made it across to the shore, and when I looked back the volcano was already rising from the lake. I could see Shandon on the isle, his arms still upraised, the smoke and the sparks coloring the air about him. I went then in search of you. After a time, I received your message."

"Was he able to use the power-pulls before this thing happened?"

"No, he could not even detect their presence."

"What of the others who have been recalled?"

"They are all of them on the isle. Several of them are drugged, to keep them tranquil."

"I see."

"Perhaps you will now change your mind and do as I suggested?"

"No."

We sat there until light came into the world about fifteen minutes later. The fog was beginning to lift, but the sky was still overcast. The sun set clouds on fire. The wind came cool. I thought of my ex-spy, playing with his volcano and communing with Belion. Now was the time to hit him, while he was still intoxicated with his new strengths. I'd have liked to draw him away from the isle, into some section of Illyria Green Green had not corrupted, where everything that lived would be my ally. He would not respond to anything that obvious, though. I wanted to get him away from the others, if possible, but I could not figure a way to accomplish it.

"How long did it take you to crap this place up?" I asked.

"I began altering this section about thirty years ago," he said.

I shook my head, stood and kicked dirt into the fire until I'd smothered it.

"Come on. We'd better get moving."

*   *   *

Ginnunga-gap, according to the Norsemen, existed in the center of all space in the morning of time, shrouded with perpetual twilight. Its northern rim was ice and its southern was flame. Over the ages, these forces fought and the rivers flowed and life stirred within the abyss. Sumerian myth has it that En-ki did battle with and subdue Tiamat, the dragon of the sea, thus separating the earth and the waters. En-ki himself, though, was sort of like fire. The Aztecs held that the first men were

made of stone, and that a fiery sky portended a
new age. And there are many stories of how a
world may end: Judgment Day, Götterdämmerung,
the fusion of atoms. For me, I have seen worlds
and people begin and end, actually and metaphor-
ically, and it will always be the same. It's always
fire and water.

No matter what your scientific background,
emotionally you're an alchemist. You live in a
world of liquids, solids, gases and heat-transfer
effects that accompany their changes of state. These
are the things you perceive, the things you feel.
Whatever you know about their true natures is
grafted on top of that. So, when it comes to the
day-to-day sensations of living, from mixing a cup
of coffee to flying a kite, you treat with the four
ideal elements of the old philosophers: earth, air,
fire, water.

Let's face it, air isn't very glamorous, no matter
how you look at it. I mean, I'd hate to be without
it, but it's invisible and so long as it behaves itself
it can be taken for granted and pretty much ignored. Earth? The trouble with earth is that it
endures. Solid objects tend to persist with a monotonous regularity.

Not so fire and water, however. They're form-
less, colorful, and they're always doing something.
While suggesting you repent, prophets very sel-
dom predict the wrath of the gods in terms of
landslides and hurricanes. No. Floods and fires are
what you get for the rottenness of your ways.
Primitive man was really on his way when he
learned to kindle the one and had enough of the
other nearby to put it out. Is it coincidence that

we've filled hells with fires and oceans with monsters? I don't think so. Both principles are mobile, which is generally a sign of life. Both are mysterious and possess the power to hurt or kill. It is no wonder that intelligent creatures the universe over have reacted to them in a similar fashion. It is the alchemical response.

Kathy and I had been that way. It had been a stormy, mobile, mysterious thing, full of the power to hurt, to give birth and to give death. She had been my secretary for almost two years before our marriage, a small, dark girl with pretty hands, who looked well in bright colors and liked to feed crumbs to the birds. I had hired her through an agency on the world Mael. In my youth, people were happy to hire an intelligent girl who could type, file and take shorthand. What with the progressive debasement of the academic machine and the upward-creep of paper-requirements in an expanding, competitive labor market, however, I'd hired her on advice of my personnel office on learning she held a doctorate in Secretarial Science from the Institute of Mael. God! that first year was bad! She automated everything, screwed up my personal filing system and set me six months behind on correspondence. After I had a twentieth-century typewriter reconstructed, at considerable expense, and she learned to operate it, I taught her shorthand and she became as good as a twentieth-century high school graduate with a business major. Business returned to normal, and I think we were the only two people around who could read Gregg scribbles—which was nice for confidential matters, and gave us something in common. Her a bright little flame and me a wet blanket, I'd reduced her to tears many times that first year. Then she became indispensable, and I realized it was not just because she was a good secretary. We were married and there were six happy years—six and a half, actually. She died in the fire, in the Miami Stardock disaster, on her way to meet me for a conference. We'd had two sons, and one of them is still living. On and off, before and since, the fires have stalked me through the years. Water has been my friend.

While I feel closer to the water than the fire, my worlds are born of both. Cocytus, New Indiana, St. Martin, Buningrad, Mercy, Illyria and all the others came into being through a process of burning, washing, steaming and cooling. Now I walked through the woods of Illyria—a world I'd built as a park, a resort—I walked through the woods of an Illyria purchased by the enemy who walked by my side, emptied of the people for whom I had created it: the happy ones, the vacationers, the resters, the people who still believed in trees and lakes and mountains with pathways among them. They were gone, and the trees among which I walked were twisted, the lake toward which I headed was polluted, the land had been wounded and the fire her blood spurted from the mountain that loomed before, waiting, as the fire always is, waiting for me. Overhead hung the clouds, and between their matted whiteness and my dirty blackness flew the soot the fire sent, an infinite migration of funeral notices. Kathy would have liked Illyria, had she seen it in another time and another place. The thought of her in this time and this place, with Shandon running the show, sickened me. I cursed softly as I walked along, and those are my thoughts on alchemy.

*   *   *

We walked for about an hour and Green Green began complaining about his shoulder and fatigue in general. I told him he could have my sympathy so long as he kept walking. This must have satisfied him because it shut him up. An hour after that, I did let him take a break while I climbed a tree to check out the forward terrain. We were getting close, and it was about to become a steady downhill hike the rest of the way in. The day had lightened as much as it was going to and the fog had vanished almost entirely. It was already warmer than it had been at any time since my landing. The perspiration rolled down my sides as I climbed and the flaky bark bit into my hands, which had grown soft in recent years. With each branch that I disturbed a fresh cloud of dust and ashes appeared. I sneezed several times, and my eyes burned and watered.

I could see the top of the isle above the fringe of distant trees. To the left of it and somewhat back, I could see the smoldering top of a fresh-grown cone of volcanic rock. I cursed again, because I felt like it, and climbed back down.

It took us about two more hours to reach the shore of Acheron.

Reflected in the oily surface of my lake were the fires and nothing more. Lava and hot rocks spit and hissed as they struck the water. I felt dirty and sticky and hot as I looked out across what remained of my handiwork. Small waves left lines of scum and black crud upon the shore. The water was spotted with clouds of such stuff heading in toward the beach. Fishes rocked belly up in the shallows, and the air smelled like rotten eggs. I sat upon a rock and regarded it, smoking a cigarette the while.

A mile out stood my Isle of the Dead, still unchanged—stark and ominous as a shadow with nothing to cast it. I leaned forward and tested the water with my finger. The lake was hot, quite hot. Far out and to the east, there was a second light. It seemed as if a smaller cone were growing there.

"I came to shore about a quarter mile to the west of here," said Green Green.

I nodded and continued to stare. It was still morning and I felt like contemplating the prospect. The southern face of the isle—the one I looked upon—had a narrow strip of beach following the curve of a cove perhaps two hundred feet across. From there, a natural-seeming trail zigzagged upwards, reaching various levels and, ultimately, the high, horned peaks.

"Where do you think he is?" I asked.

"About two-thirds of the way up, on this side," said Green Green, "in the chalet. That is where I had my laboratory. I expanded many of the caves behind it."

A frontal approach was almost mandatory, as the other faces of the isle possessed no beaches and rose sharply from the water.

Almost, but not quite.

I doubted that Green Green, Shandon or any-

body else was aware that the northern face could
be climbed. I had designed it to look unscalable,
but it was not all that bad. I had done it just
because I like everything to have a back door as
well as a front door. If I were to employ that
route, it would require my ascending all the way
and coming down toward the chalet from above.

I decided I would do it that way. I also decided
that I would keep it to myself until the last minute. After all, Green Green was a telepath, and for
all I knew, the story he'd given me could be a line
of *rouke* manure. He and Shandon could be working together, and for that matter there might not
even be a Shandon. I wouldn't have trusted him
worth a plugged nickel, back when they still had
nickels to plug.

"Come on," I said, rising and flipping my cigarette into the cesspool my lake. "Show me where
you left the boat."

So we made our way to the left, along the
shoreline, to the place where he remembered
beaching the thing. Only it was not there.

"Are you sure this is the place?"

"Yes."

"Well, where is it?"

"Perhaps it was loosened by one of the shocks
and drifted away."

"Could you swim as far as the isle, bad shoulder
and all?"

"I am a Pei'an," he replied, which meant he
could damn well swim the English Channel with
two bum shoulders, then turn around and go back
again. I'd only said it to irritate him.

". . . But we won't be able to swim to the isle," he added.

"Why not?"

"There are hot currents from the volcano. They are worse farther out."

"Then we are going to build a raft," I said. "I'll cut the wood with my pistol while you locate something suitable for binding it together."

"Such as?" he inquired.

"You're the one who screwed up this forest," I told him, "so you know it better than I do now. I've seen some tough-looking vines, though."

"They are somewhat abrasive," he said. "I will need your knife."

I hesitated a moment.

"All right. Here."

"Waters can come over the edges of a raft. They may be very warm."

"Then the waters must be cooled."

"How?"

"Soon it will begin to rain."

"The volcanos—"

"There won't be that much water."

He shrugged, nodded and went off to cut vines. I felled and stripped trees, perhaps six inches in diameter, ten feet in length, paying as much attention as possible to my back.

Soon it began to rain.

For the next several hours, a steady, cold drizzle descended from the heavens, drenching us to the skin, poking holes in Acheron, washing some of the filth from the shrubbery. I shaped two broad paddles and cut us a pair of long poles while I waited for Green Green to harvest sufficient cordage to bind things. While I was still waiting, the ground heaved violently and a terrific eruption split the near side of the cone halfway up. A river the color of sunsets poured from the gap. My ears rang for minutes after the explosion. Then the surface of the lake picked itself up and rushed toward me—a baby tidal wave. I ran like hell and climbed the highest tree in sight.

The water reached the base of the tree, but did not get much higher than a foot. There were three such waves in twenty minutes; then the waters began to recede, trading me a lot of mud for the timber I'd cut, plus both oars.

I grew angry. I knew my rain could not put out his bloody volcano, might even exacerbate things a bit . . .

But I was mad as hell, seeing all that work washed away.

I began to speak the words.

From somewhere, I heard the Pei'an calling. I ignored him.

After all, I wasn't exactly Francis Sandow at that point.

I dropped to the ground and felt the tug of a power-pull from several hundred yards to my left. I moved in that direction, climbing a small rise to reach its nexus. From that point, I had a clear line of vision across the bothered waters out to the isle itself. Perhaps my visual acuity had increased. I saw the chalet quite clearly. I fancied that I also detected a movement of sorts at the place where the rail guarded the end of the courtyard that overlooked the waters. Human eyes are not as

acute as a Pei'an's. Green Green had said he'd
seen Shandon clearly after crossing over the waters.

I felt her pulse as I stood there above one of
Illyria's larger veins or smaller arteries, and the
power came into me and I sent it upward.

Soon the drizzle became a heavy downpour, and
when I lowered my upraised hand the lightning
flashed and the thunders skated round and round
in the tin drum of the sky. A wind, sudden as a
springing cat and cold as the Arctic's halations,
struck me in the back and shaved my cheeks as it
passed.

Green Green cried out again. From somewhere
off to my right, I think.

Then the heavens began to sizzle, and they sent
down rains so heavily that the chalet vanished
from sight and the isle itself faded to a gray outline. The volcano was the faintest of sparks above
the water. Soon the wind raced by like a freight
train and its howling joined with the thunders to
create a perpetual din. The shores of Acheron
lengthened and the waters were buffeted until they
moved, in waves like the ones we had received, back
in that direction from which they had come. If
Green Green called out again, I could not hear him.

The water ran in rivers through my hair, down
my face and neck. But I did not need my eyes to
see. The power enfolded me and the temperature
plummeted; the rain came in sheets that cracked
like whips now; the day grew dark as night. I
laughed, and the waters rose up in spouts and
swayed like genies, and the lightnings ran their
gauntlets again and again, but the machine never
said "Tilt."

Stop it, Frank! He will know you are here! came the thoughts, addressed to that part of me which Green Green wished to address.

He does already, doesn't he? I might have replied. *Take cover till this is over. Wait!*

And as the waters came down and the winds went forth, the ground began to rock beneath me once again. The spark that hovered before me grew and glowed like a buried sun. Then the lightnings walked about it; they tickled the top of the isle; they wrote names upon the chaos, and one of them was mine.

I was thrown to my knees by another shock, but I stood again and raised both arms.

. . . And then I stood in a place that was neither solid, liquid nor gaseous. There was no light, nor was there darkness. It was neither hot nor cold. Perhaps it lay within my own mind, and perhaps not.

We stared at one another, and in my pale green hands I held a thunderbolt at port arms.

He was built like a wide, gray pillar, was covered with scales. He'd a snout like a crocodile, and his eyes were fiery. His three pairs of arms assumed various attitudes as we spoke. Otherwise he, also, did not move from where he stood.

Old enemy, old comrade . . . he addressed me.

Yes, Belion. I am here.

. . . *Your cycle has ended. Save yourself the ignominy of ruin at my hands. Withdraw now, Shimbo, and preserve a world you made.*

I doubt the world shall be lost, Belion.

Silence.

Then, *Then there must be a confrontation.*

. . . Unless you yourself choose to withdraw.
I will not.
Then there will be a confrontation.
He sighed a flame.
So be it.
And he was gone.

. . . And I stood atop the small hill and lowered my arms slowly, for the power had gone out of me.

It was a strange experience, unlike anything I had known before. A waking dream, if you would. A fantasy born of tension and anger, if you wouldn't.

The rain was still descending, though not with its previous force. The winds had lost something of their intensity. The lightnings had ceased, as had the trembling of the ground. The fiery activity had diminished, shrinking the orange nest atop the cone, stopping the wound in its side.

I stared at all this, feeling once again the wetness and the coldness and the firmness of the ground beneath my feet. Our long-distance battle had been cut short, our powers canceled. This was fine with me, though; the waters looked cooler and the slick, gray isle less forbidding.

Ha!

In fact, as I watched, the sun broke through the clouds for a moment and a rainbow unrolled itself amidst sparkling droplets, arcing through the air now clean and framing Acheron, the isle, the smoldering cone like a picture within a gleaming paperweight, miniature, contained and more than slightly unreal.

I departed the hillock and returned to the place I had left. There was a raft that needed building.

VII

As I LAMENTED my missing cowardice—it had been such a lifesaving virtue in the past—it responded by rushing back and leaving me scared as hell once again.

I'd lived far too long, and with every day that passed the odds kept growing against my lasting much longer. Although they didn't put it quite that way when giving the sales pitch, my insurance company's attitude is reflected in the size of the premiums involved. Their computer classified me along with terminal xenopath cases, according to their rates and my spies. Comforting. Probably right, too. This was the first piece of dangerous business I had been out on in a long while. I felt out of practice, though I was not sorry I had skimped. If Green Green noticed that my hands were shaking, he made no comment. They held his life, and he felt badly enough about this as it was. He was in a position now to kill me any time he wanted, if you stop to think about it very carefully. He knew it. I knew it. And he knew I knew it. And . . .

The only thing that was holding him back was the fact that he needed me to get him off of Illyria—which, logically, meant that his ship was on the isle. Which, by extension, meant that if Shandon had a ship at his disposal, he could come looking for us by air, despite our hallucinatory companions' feelings with respect to a confrontation. Which meant that we would be better off working under the trees than on the beach, and that our voyage required the cover of night. Accordingly, I moved our project inland. Green Green thought this a very good idea.

The cloud cover cracked that afternoon as we assembled the raft, but it did not break completely. The rain continued, the day grew a bit brighter, and two white, white moons passed overhead—Kattontallus and Flopsus—lacking only grins and eye-sockets.

Later in the day a silver insect, three times the size of the *Model T* and ugly as a grub, left the isle and circled the lake six times, spiraling outward, then inward. We were under a lot of foliage, burrowed our ways beneath more, stayed there until it returned to the isle. I clutched my ancient artifact the while. The bunny did not sell me out.

We finished the raft a couple hours before sundown and spent the balance of the day with our backs against the boles of adjacent trees.

"A penny for your thoughts," I said.

"What is a penny?"

"An ancient monetary unit, once common on

my home planet. On second thought, don't take me up on it. They're valuable now."

"It is strange to offer to buy a thought. Was this a common practice among your people, in the old days?"

"It had to do with the rise of the merchant classes," I said. "Everything has a price, and all that."

"That is a very interesting concept, and I can see how one such as yourself could well believe in it. Would you buy a *pai'badra?*"

"That would be barratry. A *pai'badra* is a cause for an action."

"But would you pay a person to abandon his vengeance against you?"

"No."

"Why not?"

"You would take my money and still seek the vengeance, hoping to lull me into a sense of false security."

"I was not speaking of myself. You know that I am wealthy, and that a Pei'an does not abandon his vengeance for any reason. —No. I was thinking of Mike Shandon. He is of your race, and may also believe that everything has a price. As I recall it, he incurred your disfavor in the first place because he needed money and did things that offended you in order to obtain it. Now he hates you because you sent him to prison and then killed him. But since he is of your race, which places a monetary value upon all things, perhaps you might pay him sufficient money for his *pai'badra* so that he will be satisfied and go away."

Buy our way out? The thought hadn't occurred

to me. I had come to Illyria ready to fight with a Pei'an menace. Now I held him in my hand and he was no longer a menace. An Earthman had replaced him as my number one enemy of the moment, and there was a possibility that this assessment was correct. We are a venal lot, not necessarily moreso than all of the other races—but certainly more than some. It had been Shandon's expensive tastes that had gotten him into a bind in the first place. Things had happened quickly since my arrival on Illyria, and strangely enough—for me and my Tree—it had not occurred to me that my money might be my salvation.

On the other hand, considering Shandon's record as a spender—a thing brought out at the first trial and at the appellate level—he went through money like a *betta splendens* through that most liquid of all alchemical elements. Say I gave him a half million in universal credit drafts. Anybody else could invest it and live on the dividends. He would go through it in a couple years. Then I would have problems again. He would have hit me this once, and he would figure he could do it again. And of course I could come through again. I could come through any time. So maybe he would not want to kill his golden goose. But then again, I'd never know for sure. I could not live with that.

Still, if he were agreeable, I could buy him off now. Then I could arrange for a team of professional assassins to take him out of the game as soon as possible.

But if they should fail . . .

Then he would be on my tail immediately, and it would be him or me again.

I turned it over, looked at it from every possible angle. Ultimately, it boiled down to one thing.

He'd had a gun with him, but he'd tried to kill me with his hands.

"It won't work with Shandon," I said. "He's not a member of the merchant class."

"Oh. I meant no offense. I still do not quite understand how these things work with Earthmen."

"You're not alone in that."

I watched the day fade away and the clouds zip themselves together once again. Soon it would be time to carry the raft to the shore and make our ways across the now temperate waters. There would be no moonlight to assist us.

"Green Green," I said, "in you I see myself, as perhaps I have become more Pei'an than Earthman. I do not think this is the real reason, however, for everything that I am now is but an extension of something that was already within me. I, too, can kill as you would kill and hold with my *pai'badra* come hell or high water."

"I know that," he said, "and I respect you for it."

"What I am trying to say is that when this thing is over, if we should both live through it, I might welcome you as a friend. I might intercede for you with the other Names, that you have another chance at confirmation. I might like to see a high priest of Strantri, in the Name of Kirwar of the Four Faces, Father of Flowers, should He be willing."

"You are trying to find my price now, Earthman."

"No, I am making a legitimate offer. Take it as you would. As yet, you have given me no *pai'badra*."

"By trying to kill you?"

"Under false *pai'badra*. This does not bother me."

"You know that I may slay you whenever I wish?"

"I know that you think so."

"I had thought this thing better shielded."

"It is a matter of deduction, not telepathy."

"You *are* much like a Pei'an," he said, after a moment. "I promise you that I will withhold my vengeance until after we have dealt with Shandon."

"Soon," I said. "Soon we shall depart."

And we sat there and waited for the night to fall. After a time, it did.

"Now," I said.

"Now," and we stood and raised the raft between us.

We carried it down to the water's edge, waded out into the warm shallows, set it a-drifting.

"Got your paddle?"

"Yes."

"Let's go."

We climbed aboard, stabilized the thing, began paddling, then poling.

"If he was above bribery," he said, "why did he sell your secrets?"

"He would have sold the others out," I said, "had my people paid him more."

"Then why is he above bribery?"

"Because he is of my race and he hates me. Nothing more. There is no buying that kind of *pai'badra*."

I thought then that I was right.

"There are always dark areas within the minds

of Earthmen," he observed. "One day I would like to know what is there."

"Me too."

A moon came up then, because a generalized blob of light appeared behind the clouds. It drifted slowly towards midheaven.

The water splashed gently beside us, and little wavelets of it struck against our knees, our boots. A cool breeze followed us from the shore.

"The volcano is at rest," he said. "What did you discuss with Belion?"

"You don't miss a trick, do you?"

"I tried to contact you several times, and I know what I found."

"Belion and Shimbo are waiting," I said. "There will be quick movements, and one of them will be satisfied."

The water was black as ink and warm as blood; the isle was a mountain of coal against the pearl and starless night. We poled until we lost the bottom, then commenced paddling, silently, twisting the oars. Green Green had a Pei'an's love of the water in him. I could feel it in the way that he moved, in the ragtails of emotion that I picked up as we proceeded.

To cross over the dark waters . . . It was an eerie feeling, because of what the place meant to me, because of the chord it had struck within me while I was building it. The feeling of the Valley of Shadows, the sense of the serene passing, this was absent. This place was the butcher's block at the end of the run. I hated it and I feared it. I knew that I lacked the spiritual stamina to ever duplicate it. It was one of those once in a lifetime creations that made me wish I hadn't. To cross over the dark waters meant to me a confrontation with something within myself that I did not understand or accept. I was cruising along on Tokyo Bay, and suddenly this was the answer, looming, the heaped remains of everything that goes down and does not come again to shore, life's giant kitchen-midden, the rubbish heap that remains after all things pass, the place that stands in testament to the futility of all ideals and intentions, good or bad, the rock that smashes values, there, signalizing the ultimate uselessness of life itself, which must one day be broken upon it, not to rise, never, no, not ever, again. The warm waters splashed about my knees, but a chill shook me and I broke rhythm. Green Green touched my shoulder, and we matched our paddling once again. —"Why did you make it, if you hate it so?" he asked me.—"They paid me well," I replied, and, "Bear to the left. We're going in the back way." Our course altered, shifting westward as he strengthened his strokes and I lightened mine. —"The back way?" he repeated. —"Yes," I said, and I did not elaborate.

As we neared the isle, I ceased my reflections and became a mechanical thing, as I always do when there are too many thoughts to think. I paddled and we slipped through the night, and soon the isle lay to starboard, mysterious lights flecking its face. From ahead, the light that glowed atop the cone crossed our path, dappling the waters, casting a faint red glow upon the cliffs.

We passed the isle then and moved toward it from the north. Through the night, I saw the northern face as in daylight. Memory mapped its scars and ridges, and my fingertips tingled with the texture of its stone.

We drew near, and I touched the sheer, black face with my oar. We held that position while I stared upward, then said, "East."

Several hundred yards later, we came to the place where I had hidden the "trail." A cleft slanted within the rock—forty feet of chimney—where the pressure of back and feet allowed ascent to a narrow ledge, along which a man might edge his way for sixty feet, to encounter a series of hand- and foot-holds leading up.

I told this to Green Green, and he stabilized the raft while I went on ahead. Then he followed, uncomplaining, though his shoulder must have been bothering him.

When I reached the top of the chimney, I looked down and was unable to spot the raft. I mentioned this, and Green Green grunted. I waited until he made it to the top, and helped him out of the cleft. Then we began inching our way along the cleft, eastward.

It took us about fifteen minutes to reach the upward trail. Again, I went first, after explaining that we had a five-hundred-foot climb before we reached another ledge. The Pei'an grunted again and followed me.

Soon my arms were sore, and when we made the ledge I sprawled and lit a cigarette. After ten minutes, we moved again. By midnight, we had made it to the top without mishap.

We walked, for about ten minutes. Then we saw him.

He was a wandering figure, doubtless narco-
tized up to the ears. Maybe not, though. You can
never be too sure.

So I approached him, placed my hand upon his
shoulder, stood before him, said, "Courtcour, how
have you been?"

He looked up at me through heavy-lidded eyes.
He weighed about three hundred fifty pounds,
wore white garments (Green Green's idea, I guess),
was blue-eyed, light-complexioned and soft-spoken.
He lisped a bit when he answered me.

"I think I have all the data," he said.

"Good," I answered. "You know that I came
here to meet this man—Green Green—in a combat of sorts. We have become allies recently, against
Mike Shandon . . . ?"

"Give me a moment," he replied.

Then, "Yes," he said. "You lose."

"What do you mean?"

"Shandon kills you in three hours and ten
minutes."

"No," I said. "He can't."

"If he does not," he replied, "it will be because
you have slain him. Then Mister Green will kill
you about five hours and twenty minutes from
now."

"What makes you so sure?"

"Green is the worldscaper who did Korrlyn?"

"Are you?" I asked.

"Yes."

"Then he will kill you."

"How?"

"Probably by means of a blunt instrument," he
said. "If you can avoid that, you might be able to

take him with your hands. You've always proven
just a bit stronger than you look, and it fools
people. I do not think it will help you this time,
though."

"Thanks," I said. "Don't lose any sleep."

". . . Unless you are both carrying secret weapons," he said, "and it is possible that you are."

"Where is Shandon?"

"In the chalet."

"I want his head. How do I get it?"

"You are a kind of demon factor. You have that
ability which I cannot fully measure."

"Yes. I know."

"Do not use it."

"Why?"

"He has one, too."

"I know that also."

"If you can kill him at all, you kill him without
it."

"Okay."

"You do not trust me."

"I don't trust anybody."

"Do you remember the night you hired me?"

"Faintly."

"It was the best meal I ever had in my life. Pork
chops. Lots of them."

"It comes back to me."

"You told me of Shimbo then. Invoke him and
Shandon will invoke the other one. Too many
variables. It may be fatal."

"Maybe Shandon has gotten to you."

"No. I am just measuring probabilities."

"Could Yarl the Omnipotent create a stone he
could not lift?" Green Green asked him.

"No," said Courtcour.

"Why not?"

"He would not."

"That is no answer."

"Yes it is. Think about it. Would *you?*"

"I do not trust him," said Green Green. "He was normal when I brought him back, but I believe that perhaps Shandon has reached him."

"No," said Courtcour. "I am trying to help you."

"By telling Sandow he is going to die?"

"Well, he is."

Green raised his hand, and suddenly he was holding my gun, which he must have teleported from my belt, in the same fashion as he had obtained the tapes. He fired twice and handed it back to me.

"Why did you do that?"

"He was lying to you, trying to confuse you. Trying to destroy your confidence."

"He was once a close associate of mine. He had trained himself to think like a computer. I think he was trying to be objective."

"Get the tape and you can resurrect him."

"Come on. I've got two hours and fifty-eight minutes."

We walked away.

"Should I not have done that?" he asked me, after a time.

"No."

"I am sorry."

"Great. Don't kill anybody else unless I ask you to, huh?"

"All right. —You have killed many people, have you not, Frank?"

"Yes."

"Why?"

"Them or me, and I'd rather it was them."

"So?"

"You didn't have to kill Bodgis."

"I thought—"

"Shut up. Just shut up."

We walked on, passing through a cleft of rock. Tendrils of mist snaked by, touched our garments. Another shadowy figure stood off to the side, at the place where we emerged upon a downward-sloping trail.

". . . Coming to die," she said, and I stopped and looked at her.

"Lady Karle."

"Pass on, pass on," she said. "Hasten to your doom. You could not know what it means to me."

"I loved you once," I said, which was not the right thing to say at all.

She shook her head.

"The only thing you ever loved—besides your-self—was money. You got it. You killed more people than I know of to keep your empire, Frank. Now there has finally come a man who can take you. I am proud to be present at your doom."

I turned on the torch and shone it upon her. Her hair was so red and her features so white. . . . Her face was heart-shaped and her eyes were green, as I remembered them. For a moment, I ached for her.

"What if I take *him?*" I asked.

"Then I'm probably going to be yours again for awhile," she replied, "but I hope not. You are evil and I want you to die. I'd find a way myself, if you were to have me again."

"Stop," said Green Green. "I brought you back from the dead. I brought this man here to kill him. I was usurped by a human being who, fortunately or unfortunately, is possessed of a similar intention with respect to Sandow. But Frank and I have our fates cast together now. Consider me. I restored you and I will preserve you. Help us to get at our enemy and I will reward you."

She moved out of the circle of light and her laughter came down upon us.

"No," she called out. "No, thank you."

"I once loved you," I said.

There was silence, then, "Could you do it again?"

"I don't really know, but you mean something to me—something important."

"Pass on," she said. "All debts be canceled. Go to Shandon and die."

"Please," I said. "Once upon a time, when I held you it meant much to me. Lady Karle, I have never stopped caring for you, even after you left. And it was not I who broke the Ten of Algol, though this is often said."

"It was you."

"I think I could convince you that it was not."

"Don't bother trying. Pass on."

"All right," I said. "I won't stop, though."

"What? Stop what?"

"Caring for you, some," I said.

"Pass on. Please pass on!"

And we did.

All that time we had been speaking her language—

Dralmin—and I hadn't even realized that I had switched from English. Funny.

"You have loved many women, haven't you, Frank?" asked Green Green.

"Yes."

"Were you lying to her—about caring for her?"

"No."

We followed the trail until I could see the lights of the chalet before/below me. We continued in that direction, and a final figure appeared, drew near.

"Nick!"

"That's right, mister."

"It's me—Frank!"

"By God, I think it is. Come closer, huh?"

"Sure. Here's a light." I spilled it all over myself so that he could see.

"Jesus! It's really you!" he said. "That guy down there is a nut, you know, and he's after you."

"Yeah, I know."

"He wanted me to help get you, and I told him to go indulge in auto-eroticism. He was mad. We had a fight. I busted his nose and got the hell out. He didn't come after me, though. He's tough."

"I know."

"I'm going to help you get him."

"Okay."

"But I don't like that guy you're with."

Nick, all out of the past and storming. . . . It was great.

"What do you mean?"

"He's the one responsible for the whole thing. He brought me back, and the others. He's a sneaky son of a bitch. If I were you, I'd take him out of the picture real quick."

"We're allies now, he and I."

Nick spat.

"I'm going to get you, mister," he said to Green Green. "When this whole thing is over, you're mine. Remember those days when you questioned me? It wasn't fun. —And now, my turn will come."

"All right."

"No, it isn't! It's not all right at all. You called me 'Shorty,' or the Pei'an equivalent thereof, you dumb vegetable! When I get my turn, I'll roast you! I'm glad I'm alive again, and I guess I owe that to you. But I'll croak you, bastard! You've got it coming, and you'd better believe it. I'll take you with anything available."

"I doubt it, little man," Green Green said.

"Let's wait and see," I said.

So Nick joined us, walking on the other side of me from Green Green.

"Is he down there now?" I asked.

"Yes. Do you have a bomb?"

"Yes."

"That would probably be the best way. Make sure he's inside and lob it in through the window."

"Is he alone?"

"Well— No. But it wouldn't exactly be murder. Once you get the tapes you can bring back the girl."

"Who is she?"

"Her name is Kathy. I don't know her."

"She was my wife," I said.

"Oh. Well, I guess that idea is out. We have to go in."

"Perhaps," I said. "If we have to, I'll take care of Shandon and you get Kathy out of the way."

"He wouldn't hurt her."

"Oh?"

"It's been several months since we woke up, Frank. We didn't know where we were or why. And this green guy said he didn't know any more about it than we did. For all we knew we were really dead. We only found out about you when he and Mike had the argument. Green dropped his guard one day and Mike picked his brains, I guess. Anyhow, Mike and the girl—Kathy, yes—sort of have a thing going between them. I guess they're in love."

"Green, why didn't you tell me this?"

"I did not deem it important. Is it?"

I didn't answer because I didn't know. I thought quickly. I leaned my back against a rock and pushed the gas pedal of my mind to the floor. I had set out to find and kill an enemy. Now he stood by my side while I sought a different enemy in his stead. Now to find out that he was shacking up with the resurrected wife I'd come to rescue . . . This did change things. How, I was not sure. If Kathy was in love with him, I was not about to burst in and shoot him down in front of her. Even if he were just using her, even if he didn't care anything for her, I could not do that—not with him meaning something to her. It seemed that Green Green's earlier suggestion was the only thing left—to contact him and try to buy him off. He had a new power and a pretty girl. Add to that a wad of money, and he might be persuaded to lay off. It still troubled me, though, that he had tried to kill me with his hands.

I could just turn around and go back. I could climb aboard the *Model T* and in less than a day be scooting toward Homefree. If she wanted Shandon, let her have him. I could settle my score with Green Green and return to my fortress.

"Yes, it is important," I said.

"Does it alter your plans?" Green Green asked me.

"Yes."

"Just because of the girl?"

"Just because of the girl," I said.

"You are a strange man, Frank, to come all this way and then change your mind because of a girl who is only an ancient memory to you."

"I have a very good memory."

I did not like the idea of leaving my Name's enemy running around in the body of a capable and clever man who would not mind seeing me dead. It was a combination that could keep me awake nights, even on Homefree. On the other hand, what good is a dead golden goose—or pigeon, as the case would be? It's funny how, if you live long enough, friends, enemies, lovers, haters move around you as at a big, masked ball, and every now and then there is some mask-switching.

"What are you going to do?" Nick asked.

"I'm going to talk to him. Make a deal if I can."

"You said he would not sell his *pai'badra*," said Green Green.

"I thought so when I said it. But this thing with Kathy now makes it necessary that I try to buy it."

"I do not understand."

"Don't try. Maybe the two of you had better wait here, in case he starts shooting."

"If he kills you, what are we to do?" asked Green Green.

"That'll be your problem then. —See you in a little while, Nick."

"Check, Frank."

I moved on down the trail, maintaining my mental shield. I used the rocks for cover, crawling among them as I neared. Finally, I lay flat on my stomach about a hundred fifty feet above the place. Two huge boulders shielded me and cast heavy shadows. I rested the pistol on my forearm and covered the back door.

"Mike!" I called out. "This is Frank Sandow!" and I waited.

Perhaps half a minute passed while he decided, then, "Yes?"

"I want to talk."

"Go ahead."

Suddenly the lights went out below me.

"Is it true what I've heard about you and Kathy?"

He hesitated, then, "I guess so."

"Is she with you now?"

"Maybe. Why?"

"I want to hear her say it."

Then, after everything, her voice:

"I guess it's true, Frank. We didn't know where we were, or anything—and I remembered that fire. . . . I don't know how to—"

I bit my lip.

"Don't apologize," I said. "That was a long time ago. I'll live."

Mike chuckled.

"You seem confident of that."

"I am. I've decided to do it the easy way."

"What do you mean?"

"How much do you want?"

"Money? You scared of me, Frank?"

"I came here to kill you, but I won't do it if Kathy loves you. She says she does. Okay. If you've got to go on living, then I want you off my back. How much will it take for you to pick up your marbles and go away?"

"What are marbles?"

"Forget it. How much?"

"I hadn't thought you would offer, so I never thought about it. A lot, though. I'd want a guaranteed income for life, a large one. Then some really large purchases in my name—I'd have to make a list. —You really do mean it? This isn't a trick?"

"We're both telepaths. I propose we drop our screens. In fact, I'd insist on it as a condition."

"Kathy has been asking me not to kill you," he said, "and she would probably hold it against me if I did. Okay. She means more to me. I'll take your money and your wife and go away."

"Thanks a lot."

He laughed.

"My luck is finally good. How do you want to handle this?"

"If you'd like, I can give you a lump sum and then have my attorneys set up a trust."

"I like. I want everything to be legal. I want a million, plus a hundred thousand a year."

"That's a lot."

"Not to you."

"Just commenting. —Okay, I agree." I wondered

how Kathy was taking all this. She could not have changed so much in a few months but that this would not sound a bit sickening to her. "Two things," I added. "The Pei'an, Gringrin-tharl—he's mine now. We have a score to settle."

"You can have him. Who needs him? —What's the other thing?"

"Nick, the dwarf, comes away with me, in one piece."

"That little—" Then he laughed. "Sure. In fact, I kind of like him. —That's all?"

"That's all."

The sun's first rays tickled the belly of the sky and the volcanos flamed like Titan torches out over the water.

"Now what?"

"Wait till I pass a message to the others," I said.

—*Green Green, he'll deal. I have his* pai'badra. *Tell Nick. We depart in a few hours. My ship will come for me later today.*

—*I hear you, Frank. We will be with you shortly.*

Now only the Pei'an remained to be dealt with. It was almost too easy. I was still on the lookout for a trick. It would have to be an awfully elaborate one, though. I was inclined to doubt the possibility of collusion between Green Green and Mike. Anyhow, I would know in a few moments, when Mike and I dropped our screens.

But after all my preparations, to settle the whole thing like a couple of businessmen . . .

I could not tell whether I had chuckled or snorted. It was something that fell somewhere in between.

Then I felt that it was wrong. It? Something, I

do not know what. It was a feeling that probably goes back to the caves or the trees. Hell, maybe even the oceans. Flopsus shone through the ash and the smoke and the mist, and she was the color of blood.

A quietness seemed to settle over everything as the breezes grew still. Then that old gut-grabbing fear was back with me again, and I fought it. A big hand was about to come down out of the sky and squash me, but I lay still. I had conquered the Isle of the Dead, and Tokyo Bay burnt all about me. Now, though, I looked down the slope into the Valley of Shadow. It is so easy for me to find things to be morbid about, and all things came to remind me of this. I shuddered and stilled my shaking. It would not do for Shandon to find fear in my heart.

Finally, after I could wait no longer, "Shandon," I said, "I'm dropping my shield. You do the same."

"All right."

. . . And our minds met, moved about inside one another.

—*You mean it*. . . .

—*So do you*. . . .

—*Then it's a bargain*.

—*Yes*.

And the "No!" that slammed back from the subterranean recesses of the world and echoed down from the towers of the sky clashed like cymbals within our minds. A flash of red heat passed through my body. Then, slowly, I stood, and my limbs were as firm as the mountains. Through lines of red and green, I saw everything as clearly as by daylight. I saw where, down below me,

Mike Shandon emerged from the chalet and slowly turned his head to rake the heights. Finally, our eyes met, and I knew then that what had been spoken or written in that place where I had stood with a thunderbolt in my hands had been true: —*Then there must be a confrontation.* Flames . . . —*So be it.* Darkness. There had been a patterning of events from the time I had departed Homefree up until this moment, which overrode, defeated the agreements of men. Ours had been a series of subsidiary conflicts, their resolution unimportant to those who controlled us now.

Controlled. Yes.

I had always assumed Shimbo to be an artificial creation, conditioned into me by the Pei'ans, an alternate personality I assumed when designing worlds. There had never been a clash of wills either. He had come only when summoned, delivered and departed.

He had never taken over spontaneously, forced any sort of control upon me. Perhaps deep down inside I wanted him to be a god, because I wanted there to be a God/god/gods somewhere and perhaps this desire was the animating force, and my paranormal powers the means for what was happening. I don't know. I don't know. . . . Once there was a burst of light when he came, so bright that I cried, not knowing why. Hell, that's no answer. I just don't know.

So we stood there regarding one another, two enemies who had been manipulated by two older enemies. I imagined Mike's surprise at this turn of events. I tried to contact him, but my faculty was completely blocked. I imagined that he was remembering that strange, earlier confrontation himself, however.

Then I saw that the clouds were massing overhead, and I knew what that meant. The ground beneath my feet gave a gentle shudder, and I knew what that meant, too.

One of us was going to die, though neither of us wished this.

—*Shimbo, Shimbo*, I said within me, *Lord of Darktree Tower, must this thing be?*

. . . And even as I said it I knew that there would be no reply, not even for me—save for what followed.

The thunders rolled, soft and long, like a distant drumbeat.

The lights out over the water grew brighter.

We stood as at the ends of a dueling field in hell, waves of light washing about us, clotted with mist, dotted with ash; and Flopsus hid her face, edging the clouds with blood.

It takes the powers a time to move, after they've been built to the proper point. I felt them pass through me from the nearest power-pull, then move away in great waves. I stood, unable to move a muscle or to close my eyes against the stare of the other. In the twisted light through which I saw, he occasionally flickered, and I glimpsed the outline of the one I had come to know as Belion.

I was diminishing and expanding, simultaneously; and long moments passed before I realized that it was I, Sandow, who was becoming more and more inert, passive, smaller. Yet, at the same time I felt the lightnings take root in my fingertips, their swaying tops high above me in the sky, waiting to be turned and prodded and drawn crashing to the ground: I, Shimbo of Darktree, Shrugger of Thunders.

The gray cone to my left was slashed down the side like an arm and its orange blood spilled forth into Acheron, to sizzle and steam in the now glowing waters; its fingers flexed high and ruddy in the night. Then I split the sky with my lines of chaos and sent them down below me in a deluge of light, as the cannons of heaven saluted and the winds of the sky rose again, and the rains came.

He was a shadow, a nothingness, a shadow, then he stood there again when the light died, my enemy. The chalet was burning behind him and something cried, "Kathy!"

"Frank! Come away!" cried the green man, and the dwarf tugged at my arm, but I brushed them both aside and took the first step toward my enemy.

A consciousness touched my own, then Belion's—for I could feel the reflex that shrugged off the latter. Then the green one cried out and drew the dwarf away.

My enemy took his first step and the ground shuddered beneath it, slipped in places, collapsed upon itself.

The winds beat at him as he took his second step, and he fell to the ground, causing fissures to open about him. I fell with my second step as the ground gave way beneath me.

As we lay there, the isle gave a shaking, shrugging twist to our shoulder of rock, and it slid and settled and smoke came up from the cracks within it.

When we rose and took our third step, we stood in a nearly level place. I shattered the rocks about him as I took my fourth step; and with his, he toppled rocks toward me from above. Five was the wind and six was the rain, and his were the fire and the earth.

The volcanos lit up the lower sky and fought with my lightnings for the upper. The winds lashed the waters below us, and we continued to sink toward them with each jogging of the isle. I heard their splashing, within the wind, the thunder, the explosions, the constant *plit-plit* of the rain. At my enemy's back, the partly crumbled chalet still burned.

With my twelfth step, the cyclones arose; and with his the entire isle began to sway and creak, the fumes coming heavier and more noxious now.

Then something touched me in a way that I should not be touched, and I looked for the cause.

The green man stood on a crag of rock, holding a weapon in his hands. A moment earlier, it had hung at my side, not to be used for the gaining of cycles such as this.

He pointed it first at me. Then his hand wavered and, before I could strike him, jerked to his right.

A line of light leaped forward and my enemy fell.

But the movement of the isle saved him. For the green man fell as it shuddered, and the weapon fell away. Then my enemy rose again, leaving his right hand on the ground beside him. He held the wrist in his left and stepped toward me.

Chasms began to open about us, and it was then that I saw the girl.

She had emerged from the burning building and edged around to the right of us, in the direction of the trail I had descended. Then she had been frozen for a time, watching our slow advance, one upon the other. Now she caught my attention as the chasm opened before her; and something cried out within my breast, for I knew that I could not reach her to save her.

. . . Then it broke, and I shuddered and ran toward her, for Shimbo was gone.

"Kathy!" I screamed, once, as she swayed and fell forward.

. . . And from somewhere Nick leaped up to the edge and seized her outflung wrist. For a moment, I thought he would be able to hold her.

For a moment. . . .

It was not a matter of his lacking the necessary strength. He had plenty of that. It was a question of weight and momentum, of balance.

I heard him curse as they fell.

Then I raised up my head and turned upon Shandon, with the death-fury lighting up my backbone. I reached for my gun and recalled, as in a dream, what had become of it.

Then the falling stones caught me and pinned me as he took another step, and I felt my right leg break beneath me as I fell. I must have blacked out for an instant, but the pain brought me back to consciousness. By then he had taken another step, which brought him very near, and the world was going to hell all around me. I looked up at the stump of his hand, at those manic-depressive eyes, at the mouth opened to finally speak or laugh; and I raised my left hand, supported it with my right and performed the necessary gesture. I screamed as my fingertip flared and his head fell from his shoulders, bounced once and rolled past me—those eyes still open and staring—and followed my wife and my best friend into the chasm below. What remained thudded to the ground before me, and I stared at it for a long while before the darkness sucked me down.

VIII

WHEN I AWOKE it was dawn and I was still being rained on. My right leg throbbed, about eight inches above the knee, which is bad—the place and the pain. The rain was only rain, though. The storm was over. The ground had stopped its shaking. When I was able to raise myself, however, I forgot my pain in a moment of shock.

Most of the isle was gone, sunken into Acheron, and what remained was unrecognizable as my handiwork. I lay perhaps twenty feet above the waterline, on a wide shelf of rock. The chalet was gone and a mutilated corpse lay before me. I turned away from it and considered my own predicament.

Then, as the torches of last night's dinner of blood still sputtered and blazed, befouling the morning sky, I reached out slowly and began removing the rocks that lay upon me, one by bloody one.

*　　*　　*

Pain and monotonous repetition of an action numb the mind, free it to wander.

Even if they had been real gods, what did it matter? What was it to me? Here I was still, right where I was born a thousand or so years before, in the middle of the human condition—namely, rubbish and pain. If the gods were real, their only relationship with us was to use us to play their games. Screw them all. "That includes you, too, Shimbo," I said. "Don't ever come to me again." Why the hell should I look for order where there wasn't any? Or if there was, it was an order that did not include me. I washed my hands in a puddle that had formed nearby. It felt good on my burnt finger. The water was real. So were earth, air and fire. And that was all I cared to believe in. Let it go with basics. Don't get cute and sophisticated. Basics are things you can feel and buy. If I could beat the Bay long enough I could corner the market on these commodities, and no matter how many Names were involved they would find all the property registered in my name. Then let them howl and bitch. I would own the Big Tree, the Tree of the Knowledge of Good and Evil. I rolled away the final stone and stretched out for a moment. I was free.

Now I had nothing to do but find a power-pull and rest until afternoon, when the *Model T* would come gliding in from the west. I opened my mind and felt one, pulsing somewhere to the left of me. When I felt stronger, I sat up and straightened my leg with both hands. When the throbbing subsided, I cut away the trouser-leg and saw that the flesh was not broken. I bound it as best I could without a splint—which wasn't very—above and below the fracture, and turned slowly, slowly, onto my stomach and hands and began crawling, just as slowly, in the direction of the pull, leaving what was left of Shandon behind me in the rain.

The going was not too bad, so long as it remained level. But when I had to pull myself up a ten-foot, forty-five degree slope, I was too beat even to curse for several minutes afterwards. The damned thing had been slippery as well as steep.

I looked back at Shandon and shook my head. It was not as if he had not known he was born to come in second. His whole life was testimony to that, poor bastard. I felt a moment's pity. He had come close to having it made. But he had come into the wrong game at the wrong time and the wrong place, like my brother, and I wondered where his head and hand lay now.

I crawled on. The power-pull was only a few hundred yards away, but I took a longer route that looked easier. One time, as I rested, I thought I heard a soft, sobbing sound. But it was gone too quickly for me to be sure.

Another time, and I heard it again, louder, coming from behind me.

I paused and waited till it came again. Then I headed toward it.

Ten minutes, and I lay before a huge boulder. It was situated at the base of a high wall of rock, and there was lots of other rubble strewn about. The muffled weeping was somewhere near. A cave seemed indicated and I did not want to waste my time exploring. So I called out:

"Hello. What's the trouble?"

Silence.

"Hello?"

Then, "Frank?"

It was the voice of the Lady Karle.

"Ho, bitch," I said. "Last night you told me to pass on to my doom. What's yours like?"

"I'm trapped in a cave, Frank. There's a rock that I can't move."

"It's a honey of a rock, honey. I'm looking at it from the other side."

"Can you get me out of here?"

"How did you get in?"

"I hid in here when the trouble started. I've tried to dig my way out, but all my nails are broken and my fingers are bleeding—and I can't seem to find any way around this stone. . . ."

"There doesn't seem to be a way."

"What happened?"

"Everybody's dead but you and me, and there is only a little piece of the isle left. It's raining on it now. It was quite a fight we had."

"Can you get me out of here?"

"I'll be lucky to get myself out of here—the condition I'm in."

"Are you in another cavern?"

"No, I'm on the outside."

"Then what do you mean by 'out of here'?"

"Off this damn hunk of rock and back to Homefree is what I mean."

"Then there is help coming?"

"For me," I said. "The *Model T* will be on its way down this afternoon. I've got it programmed."

"The equipment aboard . . . Could you blast the rock, or the ground beneath it?"

"Lady Karle," I said, "I've got a busted leg, a paralyzed hand and so many sprains, strains, abrasions and contusions that I haven't even bothered counting them. I'll be lucky to get the thing going before I pass out and sleep for a week. I gave you a chance last night to be my friend again. Do you remember what you said to me?"

"Yes. . . ."

"Well now it's your turn."

I moved myself back on my elbows and began to crawl away.

"Frank!"

I did not reply.

"Frank! Wait! Do not go! Please!"

"Why not?" I cried.

"Do you remember what you said to me then, last night . . . ?"

"Yes, and I remember your reply. All of that was last night, anyhow, when I was somebody else. —You had your chance and you blew it. If I had the strength, I would scratch your name and the date on the stone. So long, it's been good to know you."

"Frank!"

I didn't even look back.

—*Your changes of character continue to amaze me, Frank.*

—*So you made it, too, Green. I suppose you're in some other damn cave and want to be dug out.*

—*No. In fact I am only a few hundred feet from you, in the direction in which you were heading. I am near the power-pull, though it can't help me now. I will call out when I hear you approaching.*

—*Why?*

—*The time is near. I will go to the land of death, and there my strength shall fail. I was hurt badly last night.*

—*What do you want me to do about it? I've got problems of my own.*

—*I want the last rite. You told me that you gave it to Dra Marling, so I know that you know the way. Also, you said that you had glitten—*

— *I don't believe in that any more. Never did. I only did it for Marling because—*

—*You are a high priest. You bear the Name Shimbo of Darktree Tower, Shrugger of Thunders. You cannot refuse me.*

—*I have renounced the Name, and I do refuse you.*

—*You said once that if I helped you, you would intercede for me on Megapei. I did help you.*

—*I know that, but now that you are dying it is too late.*

—*Then give me this thing instead.*

—*I will come to you and give you what aid and comfort I can, save for the last rite. I am finished with such things, after last night.*

—*Come to me, then.*

So I did. By the time I reached him, the rain had just about let up. Too bad. It had been doing a fair job of washing away his body fluids. He had propped himself back against a rock, and the whiteness of bone shone through flesh in four places that I could see.

"The vitality of a Pei'an is a fantastic thing," I said. "You got all that in that fall last night?"

He nodded, then—*It hurts to speak, so I must*

continue in this fashion. I knew you still lived, so I kept myself alive until I could reach you.

I managed to get what was left of my pack off my back. Then I opened it.

"Here, take this. It is for pain. It works for five races. Yours is one."

He brushed it aside.

—I do not wish to dull my mentality at this point.

"Green, I am not going to give you the rite. I will give you the *glitten* root and you can take it yourself if you wish. But that's all."

—Even if I can give you that which you most desire in return?

"What?"

—All of them, back again, with no memory of what has happened here.

"The tapes!"

—Yes.

"Where are they?"

—A favor for a favor, Dra Sandow.

"Give them to me."

—The rite . . .

. . . A new Kathy, a Kathy who had never met Mike Shandon, my Kathy—and Nick, the breaker of noses.

"You drive a hard bargain, Pei'an."

—I have no choice—and please hurry.

"All right. I'll go through with it, this one last time. —Where are the tapes?"

—After the rite has begun and may not be stopped, then I will tell you.

I chuckled.

"Okay. I don't blame you for not trusting me."

—You were shielding. You must have been planning to trick me.

"Probably. I'm not really sure."

I unwrapped the *glitten*, broke off the proper proportions.

"Now we will walk together," I began, "and only one of us two will return to this place . . ."

*   *   *

After a cold, gray time and a black, warm one, we walked in a twilit place without wind or stars. There was only bright green grass, high hills and a faint aurora borealis that licked at the grayblueblack sky, following the entire circle of the broken horizon. It was as if the stars had all fallen, been powdered, were strewn upon the hilltops.

We walked effortlessly—almost strolling, though with a purpose—our bodies whole once more. Green was at my left hand, among the hills of the *glitten*-dream—or was it a dream? It seemed true and substantial, while our broken, tired carcasses lying on rocks in the rain now seemed a dream remembered, out of times long gone by. We had always been walking here, so, Green and I—or so it seemed—and a feeling of well-being and amity lay upon us. It was almost the same as the last time I had come to this place. Perhaps I had always really been here.

We sang an old Pei'an song for a time, then Green said, "I give you the *pai'badra* I held against you, *Dra*. I hold it no more."

"This is good, *Dra* tharl."

"I promised, too, to tell you something. It was

of the tapes, yes. —They lie beneath the empty green body I was privileged to wear for a time."

"I see."

"They are useless. I called them to me there with my mind, from a vault where I had kept them. They had been damaged by the forces let loose upon the isle; and so, also, were the tissue cultures. Thus do I keep my word, but poorly. You gave me no choice, though. I could not come this way alone."

I felt that I should be upset, and knew that for a time I could not be.

"You did what you had to," I felt myself saying. "Do not be troubled. Perhaps it is better that I cannot recall them. So much has gone by since their times. Perhaps they would have felt as I once felt, lost in a strange place. They might not have gone on as I did, to embrace it. I do not know. Let it be as it is. The thing is done."

"Now I must tell you of Ruth Laris," he said. "She lies in the Asylum of Fallon in Cobacho, on Driscoll, where she is registered as Rita Lawrence. Her face has been altered, and her mind. You must remove her and hire doctors."

"Why is she there?"

"It was easier than bringing her to Illyria."

"All this pain which you caused meant nothing to you, did it?"

"No. Perhaps I had worked with the stuff of life too long . . ."

". . . And poorly. I am inclined to think it was Belion within you."

"I did not wish to say it, because I did not want to offer excuses, but I feel this way also. This is why I tried to kill Shimbo. It was this part of me that you faced, and I wished to strike at it, too. After he left me for Shandon, I felt remorse for many of the things I had done. He had to be sent away, which is why Shimbo of Darktree came. Belion could not be permitted to create more worlds of cruelty and ugliness. Shimbo, who cast them like jewels into the darkness, sparkling with the colors of life, had to confront him once again. Now that he has won, there will be more such as these."

"No," I said. "We can't operate without each other, and I've resigned."

"You are bitter over all that has happened, and perhaps justly so. But one does not easily abandon a calling such as yours, *Dra*. Perhaps with the passage of time . . ."

I did not answer him for my thoughts had turned inward again.

The way that we walked was the way of death. However pleasant it seemed, this was a *glitten* experience; and while ordinary people may become addicted to *glitten* because of the euphoria and the brain-bending, telepaths use *glitten* in special ways.

Used by a single individual, it serves to heighten his powers.

Used by two persons, a common dream will be dreamed. It, also, is always a very pleasant dream—and among Strantrians it is always the same dream, because this form of religious training conditions the subconscious to produce it by reflex. It is a tradition.

. . . And two dream it and only one awakens.

It is, therefore, used in the death rite, so that

one need not go alone to the place I've spent over a thousand years avoiding.

Also, it is used for dueling purposes. For, unless agreed upon and bound by ritual, it is only the stronger who comes back. It is the nature of the drug that some sleeping parts of the two minds are set in conflict, though the conscious portions be all unaware of this.

Green Green had been so bound, so I did not fear a last-ditch trick for the gaining of Pei'an vengeance. Also, even if it were a dueling situation, I did not feel that I had anything to fear, considering his condition.

But as we walked along, I considered that I was probably hastening his death by several hours, under guise of a pleasant, near-mystical ritual.

Telepathic euthanasia.

Mental murder.

I was glad to be able to help a fellow creature shuffle off in such a decent way, on the condition that he wanted it. It made me think of my own passing, which I am certain will not be a pleasant one.

I have heard people say that no matter how much you love living, now, this minute, and think that you would like to live forever, someday you will *want* to die, someday you will pray for death. They had pain in mind when they spoke. They meant they would like to go pretty, like this, to escape.

I do not expect to go pretty, gentle or resigned into this good night myself, thank you. Like the man says, I intend to rage against the dying of the light, fighting and howling every damn step of the way. The disease that was responsible for my making it this far involved quite a bit of pain, you might even say agony, and for a long while, before they froze me. I thought about it a lot then, and I decided I would never opt for the easy way out. I wanted to live, pain and all. There's a book and a man I respect: André Gide and his *Fruits of the Earth*. On his deathbed he knew he had only a few days left and he wrote like blue blazes. He finished it in about three days and died. In it, he recounts every beautiful thing about the permutations of earth, air, fire and water that surrounded him, things that he loved, and you could tell that he was saying goodbye and did not want to go, despite everything. That is how I feel about it. So, in spite of my involvement, I could not sympathize with Green's choice. I would rather have lain there, broken-boned and all, feeling the rain come down upon me and wondering at it, regretting, resenting a bit and wanting a lot. Maybe it was this, this hunger, that allowed me to learn worldscaping in the first place—so that I could do it all myself, so that I could make more of it. Hell.

We mounted a hill and paused on its summit. Even before we reached it, I knew what would be there when we looked down the far slope.

. . . Beginning between two massive prows of gray stone, with a greensward that started out as bright as that beneath our feet and grew darker and darker as I swept my eyes ahead, there was the place. It was the big, dark valley. And suddenly I was staring into a blackness so black that it was nothing, nothing at all.

"Another hundred steps will I go with you," I said.

"Thank you, *Dra*."

And we descended the hillside, moved toward the place.

"What will they say of me on Megapei when they hear that I am gone?"

"I do not know."

"Tell them, if they ask you, that I was a foolish man who regretted his folly before he came to this place."

"I will."

"And . . . "

"That, too," I said. "I will ask that your bones be taken into the mountains of the place that was your home."

He bowed his head.

"That is all. You will watch me walk on?"

"Yes."

"It is said that there is a light at the end."

"So is it said."

"I must seek it now."

"Walk well, *Dra* Gringrin-tharl."

"You have won your battles and you will depart this place. Will you cast the worlds I never could?"

"Maybe," and I stared into that blackness, *sans* stars, comets, meteors, anything.

But suddenly there was something there.

New Indiana hung in the void. It seemed a million miles away, all its features distinct, cameo-cut, glowing. It moved slowly to the right, until the rock blocked it from my view. By then, however, Cocytus had come into sight. It crossed, was followed by all the others: St. Martin, Buningrad,

Dismal, M-2, Honkeytonk, Mercy, Summit, Tangia, Illyria, Roden's Folly, Homefree, Castor, Pollux, Centralia, Dandy, and so on.

For some stupid reason my eyes filled with tears at this passage. Every world I had designed and built moved by me. I had forgotten the glory.

The feeling that had filled me with the creation of each of them came over me then. I had hurled something into the pit. Where there had been darkness, I had hung my worlds. They were my answer. When I finally walked that Valley, they would remain after me. Whatever the Bay claimed, I had made some replacements, to thumb my nose at it. I had done something, and I knew how to do more.

"There *is* a light!" said Green, and I did not realize that he had been clutching my arm, staring at the pageant.

I clasped his shoulder, said, "May you dwell with Kirwar of the Four Faces, Father of Flowers," and I did not quite catch his reply as he drew away from me, passed between the stones, walked the Valley, was gone.

I turned then and faced what had to be the east and began the long walk home.

Coming back. . . .

Brass gongs and polliwogs.

I was stuck to a rough ceiling. No. I was lying there, face up on nothing, trying to support the world with my shoulders. It was heavy and the rocks poked, gouged. Below me lay the Bay, with its condoms, its driftwood, its ropes of seaweed, empty dories, bottles and scum. I could hear its distant splashing, and it splashed so high that it kept striking my face. There it was, life, slopping, smelling, chilly. I had had a real wild romp through its waters, and now as I looked down upon it I felt myself falling once more, falling back toward its shallows. Maybe I heard bird-cries. I had walked to the Valley and now I was returning. With luck I would evade the icy fingers of the crumbling hand once more. I fell, and the world twisted about me, resolved itself into what it had been when I left it.

The sky was bleak as slate and streaked with soot. It oozed moisture. The rocks dug into my back. Acheron was pocked and wrinkled. There was no warmth in the air.

I sat up, shaking my head to clear it, shivered, regarded the body of the green man that lay beside me. I said the final words, completing the rite, and my voice shook as I said them.

I rolled Green's body into a more comfortable-looking position and covered it with my flimsy. I picked up the tapes and their bio-cylinders which he had been concealing beneath him. He had been right. They were ruined. I placed them in my knapsack. At least Earth Intelligence would be happy with this state of affairs. Then I crawled on to the power-pull and waited there, raising a screen of forces to attract the *T*, and watching the sky.

I saw her walking, walking away, her neat hips sheathed in white and swaying slightly, her sandals slapping the patio. I had wanted to go after her, to explain my part in what had happened. But I knew it would do no good, so why lose face? When a fairy tale blows up and the dream dust settles and you find yourself standing there, knowing that the last line will never be written, why not omit any exercises in futility? There had been giants and dwarves, toads and mushrooms, caves full of jewels and not one, but ten wizards. . . .

I felt the *Model T* before I saw it, when it locked with the power-pull.

Ten wizards, financial ones, the merchant barons of Algol . . .

All of them her uncles.

I had thought that the alliance would hold, sealed as it was with a kiss. I had not been planning a doublecross, but when it came from the other side something had to be done. It was not all my doing either. There was a whole combine involved. I could not have stopped them if I had wanted to.

I could feel the *T* homing in now. I rubbed my leg above the break, hurt it, and stopped.

Business arrangement to fairy tale to vendetta. . . . It was too late to recall the second phase of that cycle, and I had just won the final one. I should have felt great.

The *T* came into view, descended quickly and hung like a world overhead as I manipulated it through the pull.

I have been a coward, a god and a son of a bitch in my time, among other things. That is one of the things about living for a very long time. You go through phases. Right now I was just tired and troubled and had only one thing on my mind.

I brought the *T* down to rest on a level space, cracked the hatch, began crawling toward it.

It did not matter now, not really, all these things I had thought when the fire was high. Any way you looked at it, it did not matter.

I made it to the ship. I crawled inside.

I fiddled with the controls and brought it to a more sensitive life.

My leg hurt like hell.

We drifted.

Then I answered us, picked up the necessary equipment, crawled outside once more.

Forgive me my trespasses, baby.

I positioned myself carefully, took aim, dissolved one big rock.

"Frank? Is that you?"

"No, just us chickens."

Lady Karle rushed out, dirty, wild-eyed.

"You came back for me!"

"I never left."

"You're hurt."

"I told you about it."

"You said you were going away, leaving me."

"You've got to learn to know when I'm being serious."

She kissed me then and helped me to stand on my one good leg, drawing my arm about her shoulders.

"Kind of like playing hopscotch," I said, as we headed for the *T*.

"What is that?"

"An old game. When I can walk again, maybe I'll teach it to you."

"Where now?"

"Homefree, where you may stay or go as you choose."

"I should have known you would not leave me, but when you said those things . . . Lords! It's a miserable day! What happened?"

"The Isle of the Dead is sinking slowly into Acheron. It's raining on it."

I looked at the blood on her hands, the dirt, then her messed hair.

"I did not mean everything that I said, you know."

"I know."

I looked all around me. Someday, I would fix it all up, I knew.

"Lords! It's a miserable day!" she said.

"Upstairs, the sun is shining. I think we can make it, if you help."

"Lean on me."

I did.

AN OFFER HE COULDN'T REFUSE

They were functional fangs, not just decorative, set in a protruding jaw, with long lips and a wide mouth; yet the total effect was lupine rather than simian. Hair a dark matted mess. And yes, fully eight feet tall, a rangy, tense-muscled body.

She clawed her wild hair away from her face and stared at him with renewed fierceness. Her eyes were a strange light hazel, adding to the wolfish effect. "What are you *really* doing here?"

"I came for you. I'd heard of you. I'm . . . recruiting. Or I was. Things went wrong and now I'm escaping. But if you came with me, you could join the Dendarii Mercenaries. A top outfit—always looking for a few good men, or whatever. I have this master-sergeant who . . . who *needs* a recruit like you." Sgt. Dyeb was infamous for his sour attitude about women soldiers, insisting that they were too soft . . .

"Very funny," she said coldly. "But I'm not even human. Or hadn't you heard?"

"Human is as human does." He forced himself to reach out and touch her damp cheek. "Animals don't weep."

She jerked, as from an electric shock. "Animals don't lie. Humans do. All the time."

"Not *all* the time."

"Prove it." She tilted her head as she sat cross-legged. "Take off your clothes."

". . . what?"

"Take off your clothes and lie down with me as *humans* do. Men and women." Her hand reached out to touch his throat.

The pressing claws made little wells in his flesh. "Blrp?" choked Miles. His eyes felt wide as saucers. A little more pressure, and those wells would spring forth red fountains. *I am about to die. . . .*

I can't believe this. Trapped on Jackson's Whole with a sex-starved teenage werewolf. There was nothing about this in any of my Imperial Academy training manuals. . . .

BORDERS OF INFINITY by LOIS McMASTER BUJOLD
69841-9 • $3.95